DRAGON HEAT

A Dragon Island Story

Jodi Kendrick

SoulGate Publishing

Dragon Heat

Copyright © 2023 by Jodi Kendrick

Published by SoulGate Publishing

First published by MT Worlds Press February 2020; Second edition published by SoulGate Publishing April 2023.

http://soulgate.org

Cover design by Dar Albert, Wicked Smart Designs

Editing by Kim Ross

Formatting by SoulGate Publishing

http://soulgate.org

Dragon Island
Dragon Heat

Enchanted Ardor
Wish

EveL Worlds : FUCN'A
Tough Nut
Diamond in the Ruff
Honeyed Nut
Gorilla in the Hiss
FUCN'A Collection One
Pedigree Collection

Finely Aged
Dragon Steel

Global Paranormal Security Agency
Awakened
Surfacing
Polestar
Aquatic Investigations
Prowler

The Kindred Chronicles
Healer
Mercenary

The Soaring Dragon Chronicles
Return Flight
Changeling

Chapter 1

The sky was a solid, perfect blue, and the sea rippled and writhed below Jori's little plane. He closed his eyes, reveling in the sun's intense brilliance on his face. Another glorious morning out over the Atlantic Ocean, flying in the general direction of Bermuda.

After setting the autopilot, and retrieving his phone from his pocket, he thumbed through icons till he found his streaming app, clipped it to the brace attached to the instrument panel next to an old photo, and began the live stream.

"Hey folks, Jori Mountainside here, checking in with a short video log while en route toward Bermuda." He relayed the date and coordinates then the events of the day and night before. "My buddy Carlos has a sick kid at home and couldn't make the trip with me. I've got a schedule to keep, so here I am flying solo in my trusty old Cessna, hoping to catch a glimpse of the legendary Beast of the Bermuda Triangle. If not, well maybe I'll find some friendly locals willing to share a beer and some local folk tales with me." He grinned. "I'll upload all the footage I can snag, and I want to thank all of you for your support and patronage—it means a lot." With a quick glance at his indicators and gages he said "I'll wrap it up here, since flying into a bird at this point would be tragic and making it home intact is always my goal, so I'll catch you all later. Peace."

Ending the recording, he checked his navigation equipment and course settings. The ocean was as vast as the sky and there was nothing otherwise visible.

He'd left Charleston with his nose pointing east, in the little Cessna he'd inherited from his mother, riding every lurch and roll of the air currents. The forecast was expected to be clear and still for days.

The Bermuda Triangle adventure was a first. He'd done the mountaineering thing, the Amazon treks and even the desert caravans. This one.... This one was dedicated to his mother.

He was out here with minimal equipment—storage space was limited, and a man did have to eat, after all. Spare batteries and solar panels powered his laptop, video and communications equipment. He had reserve gas for the generator in case of emergency, but he was determined to rely only on the power of wind and sun where possible.

This particular project, he hoped, would be the big one that brought him the recognition his father was waiting for. He certainly wasn't impressed with his achievements to date.

It didn't matter that he had thousands following his video channel, or various social media platforms with impressive funding subscriptions. It was due to these supporters that he was exactly where he was out in his little plane over the vast Atlantic Ocean. And he was determined not to let them down.

Maybe he should have held back the trip till Carlos could fly with him.

What difference did it really make? A second person in the cockpit couldn't really do much. If he was going to run into trouble, better Carlos wasn't part of it; after all, he did have a kid at home.

Every time he did one of these journeys, the doubt set in about mid-way to the target destination. That's how he knew he was getting closer.

"Alright Ma, let's find those beasties you used to tell me about."
He passed a hand over the colorful abstract tattoo on his forearm and
glanced at her picture taped to the control panel next to his phone.
When he was alone, he talked to his mother like she was next to him.
He hadn't seen her in almost two decades—since she mysteriously
disappeared, but he kept her close. It seemed the longer and tighter he
tried to hang on to her fading voice, the stronger and louder his father's
became. Telling him he was wasting his life chasing myths instead of
finishing his degree.

"Maybe I'll find myself a little island woman and settle down among
the palm trees, drinking from coconuts."

He sighed and turned to observe a different slice of the open ocean.
Nothing to do but stare and think.

Of course, he questioned the sanity of his adventures, especially
went he went out alone. He was determined to do it, regardless, and
frankly, despite his father's misgivings, he was doing just fine. The
documentaries were popular and once the books were put together,
they'd sell, too. They always did.

"I get his perspective." The old way of doing things. "Go to school,
get your education, work," he grumbled. There wasn't much room in
between. Adventures were vacations.

"I can't be a tenured professor like him, Ma." he shuddered at the
thought of being confined to stale classrooms day after day, trapped
inside, unable to see the open sky and stars. Rolling his shoulders, he
reached for his phone and turned on the music app, making sure it was
loud enough to drown out his thoughts.

He was making good time, the winds were steady, some white caps
curling on wave tips below him.

During a rather impressive chorus rendition, the music stuttered
and failed, leaving him alone with his voice over the empty ocean.

Checking the phone, the screen flickered several times, then seemed to freeze. None of the apps would open, nor could he restart the phone. "Damn." Movement on the control panel pulled his attention. The navigation indicators were also failing, as was the communications equipment when he tried to radio out.

He suddenly wondered if maybe he really should have set aside his nostalgia and updated his mother's vintage Cessna.

Without the equipment, he couldn't be sure he wouldn't overshoot the little island of Bermuda.

"Shit."

Opening the steel lock box bolted to the floor between the seats, he pulled out the manual compass he always traveled with. The needle spun.

"Fuck."

M agic flowed around Kymri as her dragon form replaced her human body. She launched into the sky, starting her next shift on patrol. As guardian commander, she was devoted to her duty, ensuring the safety of her queen and people.

The air was thick with the scent of storm and the increased winds challenged the strength of her wings.

Good. She needed to burn off her anger.

Flexing her wings with a grunt, she adjusted her tilt, soaring over the open ocean.

She had to stop letting her mother get under her scales; it wrecked her concentration.

Kolina had come into her office, again, to push her agenda and had had the gall to recruit a cousin to back her up. Kymri wasn't interested in having children at this time, she was determined to focus her time and energy on her job, regardless of how much her mother was pushing her into motherhood.

"What's suddenly bringing this on?" Kymri demanded of her mother, dropping the report she'd been reviewing on the surface of her desk.

"It's time. You're not a youngling anymore," Kolina said, then had gone tight-lipped.

Kymri's older cousin Zayli butted in, "Do your duty like the rest of us. Have your young, move on."

"This has nothing to do with you." Kymri snapped.

"It has everything to do with everyone," Zayli countered.

Kymri's eyes narrowed on her cousin, "Everyone who wants my position?"

Zayli scowled, but it was Kolina that answered, "That's of no matter. What matters is that each dragoness has her duty to fulfill and you've yet to do yours."

"I am very dedicated to my duty," Kymri growled.

"Not all of it."

"It's not complicated, Kymri, just go to the continent, find a reasonably equipped male, stay until you're sure the coupling took hold or until you can't stand him any longer, or find another until the job is done."

"Shut it, Zayli. I said this is none of your business."

"Sustaining the lineages is everyone's business, Kymri; don't be so damned selfish."

"Zayli, that will do, I'll catch up with you on the reports in my office."

Apparently, Zayli was there to bluntly make Kolina's argument for her so she could smooth things over. Good dragon, bad dragon games.

Kymri crossed her arms over her chest, "I don't have time for this; I have work do to."

"As do I, so stop wasting my time by making me have to come all the way out here from the queen's lair to talk to you about this."

"Just don't bother and leave me alone about it. I'll do it when I'm ready."

"No one has the luxury of waiting until they're ready. Especially not metal dragons, Kymri. I've been more patient with you than most."

Kymri snorted, rolling her eyes.

But her mother's stare hadn't wavered, her expression growing more intense.

"What's this really about?"

Her mother blinked, a flash of vulnerability, then the intensity shuttered back into place.

"I'm making arrangements for down time for you in the next cycle. Go to the continent. Go to Black River if you want, see the broader world. Just come back with a youngling."

"Mother, I don't want—"

"I know," she cut in. "Neither did I."

Kymri stepped back like she'd been slapped. She'd always suspected, but it was the first time Kolina said it outright.

Kolina must have seen her reaction because as she stepped toward Kymri, her expression softened, "But that doesn't mean anything. That was before. After," she shrugged, "is different."

"You never talk about him," Kymri said.

Kolina stilled, searching Kymri's face. Calculating. Would telling Kymri of her sire give her the edge she needed to convince her?

Kolina's thoughts were clear with every shift of expression.

"Never mind," Kymri said, "my next patrol shift is about to start."

She turned her back on her mother.

Kymri flew hard, tilting and dipping as the air slid around her sleek form. Metal dragons were built for speed. Her scales reflected the sunshine, making her glitter like the rippling sea below her.

A perfect day for patrols.

The further away from the main island and its peripheral islands she flew, the more her mother's hold on her psyche weakened.

I don't need offspring.

Her gaze dropped to the pelicans soaring below her, watching them a few moments to absorb their serenity. Breathing deeply of the sea air currents, she shook herself out from her head down through her body, letting it ripple out through her tail. Then she pulled her wings in, barrel-rolled and rebalanced on a lower current, swooping low over the waves.

Aligning one wingtip with the islands, she glanced off the other, searching the horizon. As a human, she never would have been able to spot the ship lingering at the edge of their territory, but in her dragon form she recognized Red's pirate ship. A thrill of excitement rippled through her. She'd pay her a visit later to see if she picked up some new cosmetics and magazines for her. Bright nail polish was one of her very few guilty pleasures. She swung her gaze away from the ship, scanning the horizon again and angled toward one of the small islands at the end of their cluster.

Each long pass around the vast islands sent her out into an ever-larger spiral right out to where Red's ship was. Extending the boundary just a little further on the next pass, she could feel the difference in the magnetic fields that protected their home from the rest of the world. Since mankind started using magnetic compasses to navigate the seas, they started finding themselves in compromised navigational troubles in the vastness of the ocean between the island of Bermuda, the Bahamas and the coast of the Americas. Unable to find their way out of the magnetic zone, they'd drift for days or be swallowed by the wild Atlantic storms. Sometimes they'd find their way to the isles of dragons, Aeleftheria Nisi. Some left with all limbs intact, many didn't.

Kymri sighed as her thoughts returned to her mother again, annoyed at how her voice just got right into her head. She loved her mother and was loyal, but they had different views on life.

The older generation. Her mother expected her to toe the line and follow tradition. Live on the island always. Live the dragon life, protect it above all else, save for the queen. As the supreme representative of their species, there was nothing above her.

Her mother wanted her to bear children, leave the Boundary Guard, and replace her in the interior Queen's Guard, so she might move onto the council in her own mother's place.

Had this been her grandmother's idea? Was her mother suddenly prompting her after pressure from her own preceding generation? Or was it just her own deep-seated ambition to get into the Queen's Council?

Kymri rolled again. She didn't care who thought she should be bearing children and giving up her role among her sister guardians. Wasn't going to happen until she was damned well ready, and that, she huffed, wouldn't be anytime soon.

Rising on a current, she flapped once or twice to climb to a new altitude. Her last pass nearly complete, a buzzing sound caught her attention.

She banked and observed the dark sky ahead. Marli had reported an incoming storm that the islands were now preparing for. It looked like a strong one. Kymri could no longer see Red's ship, likely having set sail for a new target. She sighed, no booty for her tonight, now she'd have to wait till Red returned.

The gusts were strengthening, forcing her to steady herself as the smattering rain began to hammer down.

She was used to unpredictable storms, and this one was rolling hard. Maintaining her course, it wasn't long before she was enveloped by frothing storm clouds. The buzzing had grown louder.

A crack of lightening knocked out her vision and hearing for a few seconds. Trying to regain control of her senses, a streak of white and blue entered her flight path from nowhere.

Banking hard, she saw the startled face of a man struggling to keep his plane under control. But it was too late. Their wingtips clipped, sending them both off kilter. Where it took Kymri a moment to right herself, she could see the plane could not and was wobbling under the pressure of the storm.

The contact had been enough to damage the vessel. The brace holding the wing cracked, then the wing itself.

He began to fall.

Chapter 2

J ori felt a distinctive shift in the wind. His eyes scanned the skies, but ahead of him all was blue and clear and as unbroken as it had been the last few days. The Cessna skipped over a trail of turbulence.

Turning his head, his stomach dropped. "Shit."

Catching dark color in his peripheral, he turned his head further, staring at the steel gray sea banded by a darker blue-black at the horizon.

It was like turning to find a fifty foot tall grizzly had snuck up behind you while taking a piss in the forest.

"Shit." He took a deep breath, "Okay." He flew into action, throwing all his loose stuff into the lock box where he kept his compass and other small valuables.

Fetching the lifejacket from the seat next to him, he slung it over his shoulders and strapped in while trying to maintain a semblance of steadiness with his hands gripping the control yoke.

The winds became more insistent, the white caps multiplying.

The ceiling of cloud slid closer; the sky spectacularly foreboding.

"Where the fuck did all that come from? The forecast was supposed to be clear for days," he muttered.

Craning his head, the sky closed in from behind, while the sea opposite was blinding as the sun glittered and shimmered over the writing surface. He eased the plane around, so the storm was at his tail. As he did so, a spot broke the horizon.

"Land," he breathed.

Snowstorms on Everest, pumas in the jungle, kodiaks in the northern wilds and sandstorms in the desert.

He *had* this.

He watched the storm closing in and glanced at the picture stuck to the control panel; his boyish self, squeezing faces with his mother.

"Is this what happened to you?"

His fingers curled around the control yoke, breath slow and steady to clear his mind. His ears were filled with the grind of the plane's engine and the growing roar of the winds. "Let's find a place to land."

As the first spatters of rain struck the plane, Jori ensured he was belted in place.

The Cessna was no longer skipping over the turbulence, it was stumbling as it was being thrust erratically by the storm clouds which crowded his plane, over taking him. In moments, the world had turned to slate.

The little patch of land disappeared. When he looked up, a crack of lightning blinded him. His vision cleared in time to see something massive and dark on a collision route with his propeller.

He jerked the control yoke, instinctively turning away from the threat. But it was too late. The plane bounced with a crack as the strut holding the wing next to him snapped. The wing cracked and was gone, and he was tumbling sickly through the air toward the maw of the sea.

I guess I don't *have this.*

Then Jori waited, bracing himself as the plane spun out of control, his gut in his throat.

I'm going to die.

His father's disapproving voice wormed into his thoughts.

"Campus definitely would have been safer." He gritted his teeth, hands strangling the yoke for control.

The plane bounced hard and he felt as though he changed direction. It happened again and again, the metal of the plane crunching with each impact. Belted to the seat as he was, he felt like a rag doll being jerked through the sky. He didn't know what he was hitting, but he kept expecting the sea to crash over his plane, swallowing both of them.

Finally, the Cessna made contact with the ocean surface, but instead of diving into the waves, they crashed along the surface, water spraying up and over the windshield and in through the open windows, rocks and mud striking the glass.

He hit something solid and then everything went black.

All he could hear was the rage of his pulse rushing in his ears.

He was no longer moving; the engine roar had gone silent. The cockpit was dark.

Holy. Fuck.

Was he dead?

Was he alive?

Jori wasn't in the pilot seat.

He had the sense that he was lying on an uneven surface.

Blinking, the battered walls of the plane came into view. He was lying across his equipment in the back of the plane.

His head pounded.

Definitely alive.

"Don't move," a husky feminine voice said.

What the fuck?

"You're injured, just rest for now," she commanded.

He glanced down the length of his body, thankful he hadn't pissed himself. Then searched the small space for the source of the voice.

A face loomed into his view. Big dark eyes, wild fiery hair plastered to her face, and bare shoulders.

His gaze drifted down the bare shoulders and arms. And bare breasts.

He was dead. Definitely dead.

But the dull pain in his head and the discomfort through the rest of his body argued otherwise.

Delusional, then.

"Who are you?"

"Just a neighbor." She smiled.

His breath caught.

His head swam as he started to black out again, "Beautiful..."

Chapter 3

What the hell *was* she doing?

Kymri really wasn't sure what had prompted her to interfere with the little plane and its occupant.

But she had, and now she needed to deal with it.

From the platform, in her dragon form, she could see the island spread out before her, the coast in the far distance. Below her, citizens were cleaning up after the storm. Trees were toppled, thatch had blown from roofs of smaller cottages, and water pooled in places that were usually dry. Most of the structures were fine, and as a whole the island had fared well, with minimal damage.

Unlike the damage the plane had sustained. In her attempts to save it, she feared she'd nearly killed the pilot, wasting her efforts.

It had been a relief to find him still strapped to his seat and his wide chest moving with shallow breaths. She didn't know what prompted her to move him, but despite her concern for his safety, she certainly noticed he was an attractive man. And bloody difficult to move within the confines of the battered plane, tall as he was.

At close proximity, his scent had filled her nose. A mixture of natural musk and whatever hygiene products he used, creating a scent uniquely his.

She prepared to go check on him; surely he'd be awake by now.

His head wound was a concern, but she was sure he would recover well enough.

She wondered if he'd remember her.

His body had radiated heat when she'd moved him; he had lean muscle beneath the warm skin, and soft hair.

She knew he would have resources on the tiny island at the tail end of Aeleftheria's archipelago, because she often spent time there. The survivor would comfortably find what he needed. The grounded plane would be more complicated.

What was he doing out there alone in a storm?

She hoped he wasn't an infiltrator. An infiltrator that she had rescued and led right to their doorstep. She huffed, stomping a foot in irritation with herself.

What was wrong with her? So distracted. Dammit.

"Kymri? You alright?" Marli's voice came from near the change room door.

She swished her tail and jerked her head affirmatively.

"Want company?"

She shook her head, but her tail curled around Marli, brushing lightly against her.

"See you when you're back, then." She patted her knee and stepped back to give her more room to take off.

Kymri took several steps and launched herself from the platform. Some of the people below looked up and waved as she passed.

She couldn't imagine herself leaving this place to go find a mate.

Now she had to go clean up her mess and figure out who this castaway was and if he was a threat to her people. If he was harmless, she could try to get him some help and send him along.

If he wasn't, she'd have to kill him.

Until she knew if he was a threat or not, she wouldn't condemn him. She wasn't archaic, despite the need to protect her queen.

However, she wasn't naive either, knowing full well what kind of atrocities humans performed on others. But then, was he even human? If he wasn't, what then? Again, she would take care of it as the need arose.

By the time her rounds brought her within sight of the little white plane, her body had released the tension of her worries. Flying high overhead, she surveyed the small island. A camp had been set up, with a fire burning in a clearing. He was resourceful and proactive.

The light was fading, which would shield her from his view, especially at this height.

Flying so that she was out of view from his camp, she descended at some distance, on the far side of the island, and shifted into human form as she crested the natural beach dunes. From there, she went for the stash. There was one on every island. Finding the right tree, she reached into a deep hollow and extracted a sack with clothing, leather sandals and a small knife. Dressing, she slung the small sack over her shoulder and started walking toward the camp end of the island.

Before entering the camp, Kymri watched the man for a little while; he seemed at peace, observing the sky. The breeze shifted and she could scent his body. Studying him, her eyes slid over his form, head back, his thick dark hair hanging behind him, the line of his jaw obscured by beard growth, the strong neck and broad shoulders. He was clearly a tall man, even seated as he was with his long lean legs outstretched.

Determined to engage and find out his purpose in their territory, she stepped forward.

H auling the last of his equipment cases into place, Jori turned to give his camp a once over. Pulling the elastic from his wrist, he tied his hair up into a loose bun so the sweat on the back of his neck could dry.

He drew several deep breaths of the moist ocean air as the sun prickled his skin.

With no idea as to how long he'd be here, it was vital to ensure he had what he needed. Even though the digital equipment had failed, essentially causing him to be stranded, he brought it into the camp anyway. Maybe something would shift, and he'd be able to get a signal out, or at least do some recording of his days on the island. You know, in case someone did come along a little too late, then they would at least know what became of him when his bones were found.

He set up was the solar panels and hooked up the communications. There was still nothing working properly. The satellite phone connected to wrong random numbers. The digital camera caught strange anomalies when you could see anything at all, and the video he shot was like looking into another place altogether. That was when stuff actually powered up. Clearly the magnetic interference was going to be a problem for his documentary work.

He sighed, rubbing a hand over his face, grazing over his whiskered jaw.

Since he had planned to visit islands along the way, he had the necessary camp gear, including a reliable tent and a bed roll. The biggest challenge had been prying open the jammed doors to get some of the cases out into the open, but he'd managed. It wasn't like he didn't have time on his hands.

Now, he sat on one of the portable chairs by the campfire he built from scavenged beach wood and decided to worry about rescue in the morning. For today it was enough that he'd survived a wild Atlantic storm. He laughed to himself. He *had* been rescued. Some ocean creature had fucking pushed his plane to safety. Elbows on knees, he leaned and placed his chin on his hand, fingers curled over his lips while staring at the exposed mess of the little Cessna.

He'd been damned lucky.

No one, absolutely No One, was going to fucking believe him. Not without footage of some kind, and if whatever caused the 'Bermuda Triangle' effect was still around him; nothing would work except maybe the film. Maybe. If— and that was a very big 'if'—the magnetic atmosphere didn't mess with the film exposure. And he wouldn't know that until he got it into a dark room back home.

His plane looked like a bloated whale belly on a sandbar.

Fingers digging into his hair, rubbing at the muscle, he wished the ache would go away.

He couldn't imagine what had stopped his spinning free fall. Whatever it was, had been large and strong. And intelligent. He was pretty sure it didn't have tentacles, so it wasn't the legendary Kraken.

At some point through all the 'holy shit what the fuck is happening during this killer storm?' his mother's stories weaseled through his consciousness.

Whatever it really was, it had saved his sorry ass.

This was the beast he'd come all the way out here to find. This was his mission.

And he'd failed to secure the valuable footage needed.

He'd hit his head hard enough he couldn't remember clearly. In fact, he'd dreamed that a beautiful woman had helped him out of his seat.

Now he understood why the world thought all those experiencers were crack pots. Because they were too busy surviving to document what was happening. All they had were the stories.

Crazy. Just fucking crazy. No one would believe it. Nor was there anyone to tell. He quickly turned his thoughts.

Of course, there *will* be. He would find a way home, he always did.

Meanwhile, the wind had calmed to a gentle breeze and the stars were growing brighter in the sky above him. Leaning back in his chair, he let his head fall back to admire them as they brightened a few at a time. This right here was a major part of why he did what he did. Being out in the world alone and being part of its beauty. He enjoyed the vibrant humanity in cities, but this was altogether something else.

As darkness deepened around him, the heat of the day dissipated, the warmth of his campfire was constant on his legs while he continued to watch the sky. The ocean haze faded out the edges, while the sky overhead was crystal clear. He wasn't an astronomer, but he could tell the stars seemed a little off. Maybe the magnetic field around here affected the view of the stars? Tilting his head at another angle, he tried to pick out familiar constellations. He didn't find them.

Huh.

That was cool.

The brighter stars formed a long curving line that reminded him of a serpent. Arched stars perpendicular made it look like wings. Like a dragon. And as the light receded and the sky was all there was, with almost no moon, colourful space dust webbed through the stars, filling in the space. It definitely looked like a dragon arching over the sky.

It reminded him of the stories his mother had told him as a child.

Maybe at some point, long ago, someone else had been here, stranded, looking up at the sky, and had let their mind go wildly creative and dreamed up a story, letting it evolve as their stay lengthened. Or maybe they too had encountered a creature like he had. The very thing he'd been looking for.

He closed his eyes, recalling the ride, and still had no idea how he wasn't now on the bottom of the Atlantic with sea creatures feasting on his remains. He honestly didn't know what had *really* happened. After he hit his head, he imagined a lot of fucked up stuff during the crash.

Jori was very lucky. He seemed to have some kind of guardian, given how often he found himself in sticky situations. He sighed. One of these days his luck may run out. However, today was not that day.

Tonight, he'd enjoy a campfire on the beach, get some shut eye and worry about it tomorrow.

He took a deep breath. Shelter done. Weapons next. One never knew if there were wild animals or aggressive locals resentful of his presence.

Tomorrow he would get to work scavenging what he would need for a potential extended stay on the island that he doubted was charted.

Yes, that's exactly what he'd do.

Okay. *I got this.*

That thought had gotten him through so many jams. It would do, again. It would have to.

"Hello." A feminine voice drifted to him over the campfire.

His eyes popped open. Did someone speak to him or had he finally hit the sanity wall? He'd explored some of the island and hadn't seen signs of habitation. Raising his head, his eyes adjusted to search the space around the campfire.

The figure of a woman came into focus on the other side of it.

"Hello?" he said.

The figure stepped forward and he shot to his feet.

"I didn't think there was anyone on this island," he blurted.

Her mouth quirked but didn't quite smile. She was lovely. Maybe it was the glow of the fire on her skin or his long, long, hours alone... No, she was gorgeous. He couldn't stop himself from looking her over, like his eyes couldn't resist drinking her in. She wore some kind of loose cotton covering that hugged her curvy body when the breeze pushed the fabric against her. Her hardened nipples beneath the thin fabric drew his attention and imagination. She looked as though his hands would be a perfect fit for her waist.

He swallowed, his eyes jumping back to her face. That kind of ogling was very rude, and he knew better. Clearing his throat, he moved around the fire, extending a hand, "Jori Mountainside".

She hesitantly extended her hand like his, looking as though she weren't sure what it meant, he shook it anyway. Her hand was small in his, yet her grasp firm.

"I'm Jori. Arrived with the storm," he said, pointing a thumb over his shoulder toward the mangled plane.

"Kymri Steelscale." Her gaze flitted to the craft, but she otherwise seemed unsurprised by his presence. Or unimpressed. He wasn't sure which. She wasn't giving him much.

He frowned.

She resembled the woman from his rescue dream.

That couldn't be. Could it?

He wasn't sure how to react to her presence, let alone her guarded interaction.

Women were usually much more friendly and welcoming. How to navigate this?

"So, you're a local?" he asked, cringing.

She nodded, her gaze studied him, and he suddenly felt exposed and vulnerable.

"Can I get you some coffee? I just finished making it."

She looked to the area he'd been sitting and saw the metal pot by the fire, a little metal cup nearby.

She nodded, "Thank you."

He let out a breath and moved to pour a cup, then held it outstretched, "It's still hot."

Her gaze dropped back to the pot beside the fire then leveled on him.

Why did she make him feel like an awkward teen again? This was embarrassing. Turning away, he retrieved his own cup and took a generous swallow. It wasn't quality coffee, but it was still coffee.

Watching him, she raised the cup to her lips and tilted, tasting the liquid, her gaze still watching him over the rim. His eyes were glued to hers, yet he noticed the bright color of her nail polish where her fingers curled around the metal cup. Her expression changed. He wasn't sure what it meant.

"Do you have radios on or near this island? I'd like to contact the mainland to get someone out to help with my plane."

She shook her head, "Not here." She didn't elaborate.

"Somewhere nearby?"

She shrugged, "Maybe."

Maybe? "What's going on here? Either there is or there isn't."

The cup lowered from her face, her hands dropping. "Why are you here?"

He frowned, "I'm stranded," he said, not sure what she was getting at. The wreck was clearly visible.

"Why were you flying over these waters?"

The hair on the back of his neck rose a little. His gaze scanned the darkness beyond the glow of the campfire. Something unseen lurked. Something dangerous was ready to pounce if he didn't choose his words carefully.

"I'm exploring."

"Why?"

"Why does it matter?" He was becoming exasperated by her blunt questions.

"This is my home."

He nodded, "If you can help me call for someone, I'll be happy to go."

"What are you looking for?"

He didn't answer for a long moment. In the end, he resorted to honesty. "I'm chasing childhood stories."

Her gaze turned curious and the tension wavered but didn't go away. She put the cup down in the sand by her feet, "Thank you for your coffee," she said, and turned back toward the darkness of the inner island.

"What about a radio?"

"I'll think about it," she said over her shoulder. The wind shifted, drawing the scent of tropical fruit across his nose, the ends of her wild hair catching in the light breeze.

"What a strange conversation."

Despite his confusion and frustration, his eyes had dropped to the small of her back, curve of her hips, and round ass. Then he noticed the belt and knife sheath it supported. He watched her go, eyes glued to the sway of her hips until the dark swallowed her. The cup in the sand was the only evidence she'd actually been there, and he wasn't already going delusional. The cup, and the uncomfortable swelling in his shorts.

Again, he felt as though his teen years had just rolled back on him where his dick seemed to be taking charge. She was hot. Odd, but hot. And he suspected she could carve him up if she wanted to.

Well, he'd just have to make sure she *didn't* want to.

For now, he collected her cup, dumped the coffee and decided to go for a late-night swim to exorcise his teenage fantasies. His gaze drifted to where she'd been standing, images of his hands firmly gripping her ass rolled through his mind and his dick bucked in protest. Too damned much time alone. Stripping, he pulled his shirt over his head and tossed it on the camp chair. His shorts and boxers followed before he waded into the warm water to wash away the cares of the day and take care of his sudden sexual needs.

Chapter 4

The next day, the woman, Kymri, appeared again at Jori's camp. The morning had been well spent swimming and exploring the island for fresh water and other supplies. He still hadn't found the village she'd wandered over from. The tracks she'd left in the sand went through a wooded area then picked up again on another section of the island then led straight to the water. She must have come from another island by boat.

The activity kept his mind and body in check. With little to do, his mind kept cycling through various topics, many of which he didn't want to think about—namely the past.

It wasn't that he didn't want to think about Kymri— she was incredibly hot—doing so didn't help his physical situation, just made it more frustrating and added to the tension of being stranded and unable to do much about it. So, he walked the island to burn off the sexual energy that riled him. He still couldn't believe how damned quickly he'd suddenly turned into an uncontrolled teenage boy. And he couldn't figure out what it was. She was a beautiful woman, yet he'd known many.

Her sudden appearance was making it difficult to focus on the mystery of his rescue. His notebook had quickly been filling up with recollections and theories. The equipment still wouldn't function properly, so the book was all he had to rely on.

He was all over the place. Recalling his mother's stories, considering the myths and legends he'd heard about the area, the conspiracy theories and the natural theories. When recalling the events from the night of the storm, he tried to stick to the facts, and they were sparse.

Among his camp gear was a fishing rod he'd made good use of. He cast the line then relaxed, watching the skies.

Periodically, a bird flew overhead. After a while, he noticed it seemed to be a repetitive thing, always the same path across the sky, never deviating in altitude or direction. An unusual species with a long tail, and he wished he had internet access to look up what it was. The tail and wingspan proportions reminded him of the constellation he saw the night before. Interesting.

He netted the fish he caught, packed up his rod, and went back to camp to try his luck in another shallow area tomorrow.

As soon as he reached the beach camp, he checked his campfire embers to ensure they were still glowing, prodded them, added another piece of driftwood, and then went to clean the fish in an area of beach he'd designated for it.

When he returned to the fire, he was startled by Kymri's presence.

After a pause, he said cheerily, "Good morning," She was dressed the same as she'd been before.

As was he, he mused, and hoped she wouldn't mind his shorts and t-shirt monotony. He'd packed light for the trip.

She inclined her head in greeting.

"Hungry?" he asked her, holding the freshly cleaned fish aloft.

She smiled, "It is generous of you to share your food."

He shrugged, "When I was young, my mother taught me the value of hospitality."

"A wise woman."

"She was," he said, moving forward to put the fish in place by the fire.

"Wait," she said, then went into the wooded area.

By the time she returned his stomach was growling and his hospitality patience was starting to ebb.

Re-emerging from the green space, she went to the water's edge, washed whatever she'd picked in the saltwater, then approached the waiting fish. Sliding the greens into the split belly, she set it closer to the heat to cook.

Jori didn't recognize what she'd put into the fish, but then he wasn't much of a cook. He was more of a grab something edible and stuff it in his pie-hole kind of guy. He just hoped she wasn't choosing this time to poison or drug him for nefarious reasons.

She didn't say anything while they waited for the fish, so he went in search of wide leaves to use as plates. From the corner of his eye, he could see her watching his every move, unable to discern her motives. Her face was unreadable. She'd probably slay him in a game of poker.

"So, is your island nearby?"

She nodded, "Yes, fairly close."

That was good to know. Would she help him? The last few hours had given him time to think. He really had no right to expect help from someone whose land he was trespassing on. For all she knew he was capable of causing irreparable damage to her and her home. She was smart to carry her knife. On the flip side, for all he knew she might be hunting dinner for her cannibalistic village.

He eyed the greens she'd stuffed into the fish. *I guess I'll soon find out.*

His mouth watered as the aroma of cooked fish filled the air, mingled with the scent of the mystery herb.

Soon, she pulled the fish from the heat and laid them out on the broad green leaves, handing one to him. "Tell me of yourself," she said.

It wasn't a polite request out of curiosity.

He eyed the fish. His stomach rumbled.

Her gaze hadn't left his, waiting.

"As I said before, I'm chasing childhood stories," he started carefully.

"What stories?" she dipped her fingers into the fish and extracted a piece.

"Legends of the ocean." His mouth watered.

"To what purpose?" The fish touched her tongue as she tested the temperature.

"To find out how much of it, if any, is true." His gaze fixated on the tip of her tongue.

"And then what? If you find truth, what will you do then?" the fish slid into her mouth and she licked her fingers.

He swallowed. Legends. He turned his attention back to his fish and quickly pulled a plump piece free of the bones and dropped it onto his tongue. Flavor exploded in his mouth and he nearly groaned. "What is that herb? It's amazing." He ate another piece.

She smiled at his pleasure, eating more of the fish from her leaf. "Your legend?"

"Right." He shrugged. "Document it and figure out what it is, if it's even real."

"And then what?" she prodded again.

He pulled his focus from the food back to her face. This was important to her. He needed to think carefully on what to say. "Then I will know the truth of a mystery." He shrugged.

Her free hand cupped the fish, she watched him carefully. "That's it. You've come all this way, alone, risking your safety. You'll search it out, find it if you can, then just turn around and go home?" her expression was dubious.

"It's what I do."

"What of all that?" her hand gestured toward the stack of equipment cases. "What's in there? Weapons? Contraband? What?" Her tone had been controlled, he felt *something* thrum through the air, he couldn't discern.

He straightened, rolling his shoulders and glared back at her. "Of course not."

Her chin lifted in disbelief. Expectation.

She was beautiful, feet planted, body rigid, fierce, still she waited.

And she was his most immediate way off this island.

He put his fish down on a flat rock by the fire pit then strode to the equipment boxes.

Flipping open the first one, he pulled out a camera.

"Show me what it does."

"I can't. None of it works properly here, just like my navigation won't work; that got me stuck here in the first place."

She considered this. "Explain its function."

"It's a camera, for taking pictures to document the journey."

She nodded.

He replaced it in the case, then opened the next one, laptop, satellite phone, personal phone, drives etc... Opening the other cases, another camera, communications, navigation, various other pieces of equipment required for traveling distances.

"All of this equipment is to document this myth you are chasing. To then share with the world."

He clicked the locks shut on the last case and turned to face her.

"If these myths you're chasing are real, what would you do if they don't want to be announced to the world?"

"Doesn't the world have the right to know the truth?"

"To what purpose?"

"It's the truth."

"To what end? What happens when the world finds out about this myth of yours and the world decides they need to come and see it, too. And what happens when they decide this myth is dangerous and come to destroy it?"

This was just supposed to be an adventure, like chasing the Loch Ness monster or Big Foot. A journey to honor his mother. A project to launch his career and land notoriety.

When he didn't respond she walked away... taking the fish with her.

Kymri left Jori standing alone in his little camp. By the time she reached her tree trunk stash, she realized she was still holding the fish. With a sigh, she finished eating it. No sense in wasting.

She stripped down, stuffed the clothing and knife in the hole and headed to the water.

He was a dragons-damned treasure hunter. She had known he was too good to be true. Should have let him drown in his stupid little plane. It would have been such a waste of all that lean muscle and amazing hair, though. She couldn't stop watching his hands and lips as he ate, imagining he was plucking and nibbling at her.

She almost wished he did have contraband or weapons. This journey he was on was far more dangerous to her people.

So why didn't she destroy him and his equipment on the spot?

Or shift and give him a taste of the legend he's looking for?

The image of him alone in the water pleasuring himself under the starlight slid into her mind. The broad shoulders, muscular arms, defined chest, narrow hips and long strong legs built for carrying a woman around, image. Desire spiked through her body even in her dragon form.

This wasn't good.

Not good at all.

She finished her patrol and reported back.

At her desk, she read the briefs from the other reports waiting for her approval. They all detailed the man's location on the island. She sighed. This will have to be resolved one way or the other, she couldn't just leave him there. If she waited too long, the matter would be brought to Council and they would decide his fate.

At least now she knew what he was doing in their territory. She could confiscate his equipment and send him on his way.

If she sent him away, would the desire also go away?

That would be fantastic. She hated being so distracted all the time. *This isn't me.*

She'd always been hyper-focused and driven. Clear.

Unable to stop thinking about him from the second she pulled open the door of his wrecked plane to ensure he was alive, his scent was unshakable, imbedded in her dragon brain.

She'd seen this before. With others. It was a heat. Was this why her mother had become more insistent? Or had the woman triggered it in some way? Could that happen? It didn't happen to everyone. She tried to think of those that it had, and what had happened to them. She swore, unable to remember who they were, it was so long ago, and her super focus on her work left her knowledge sparse when it came to social connections outside her small guardian circle. She knew who key figures were, but she wasn't like her mother, who knew who everyone on the island was.

Kymri was anti-social, her mother had said. She needed to mingle more, make friends and more acquaintances, she said.

Realizing her mind had gone on another tangent, she slammed the reports down on the thick surface and got to her feet.

Kolina must have triggered whatever was happening to her. Did she know about the man on the beach? Maybe she saw an opportunity and it was bloody well working out to her agenda. She didn't realize she was pacing until she found herself in front of her window staring at the tower across the city where her mother resided with the Queen's Guard.

She was on the brink of going over there to demand Kolina remove whatever dragon witchery she'd cast on her when a little voice at the back of her mind stayed her.

What if she hadn't?

Kymri would die before she gave her mother the satisfaction of knowing what was happening to her. *If* this was what was happening—a heat—she had to deal with it on her own.

She needed to visit the archive. Everything known to dragon kind was in the archive; there would be something in there. There had to be. There would be.

She nearly collided with Marli on her way out of the office, "Kymri, there you are, I have some more reports for you to review and-"

"Put them on the desk."

"But I—"

"I'll be back soon."

"It's—"

"Can wait." She said from mid-way down the corridor.

"Are you alright?"

"Fantastic." She called back when she reached the curving stone stairs. "Going to the archive."

"Do you even know where it is?" Marli's voice drifted down the stairs after her.

Chapter 5

Jori was already tiring of fish, even with the mystery herb Kymri had introduced him to. Still, he refused to raid the supply from the plane in case he needed it. He hadn't found anything other than coconuts on the island yet. The snails he was keeping as bait for the fish. He loved escargot, but without the garlic, mushrooms and butter, it just wasn't the same.

Each of the days following Kymri's last visit he went to the place where her footprints disappeared into the ocean. He watched the horizon, fishing while he did so, since he needed to eat anyway. All he saw were the endless rolling waves and the regular mystery bird flying overhead.

This time when she came, he'd be ready. Without knowing which way to go, it made no sense to take her boat. He'd have to subdue her and make her direct him to her island.

This is stupid.

He had no idea how much longer she'd let him rot here.

He had, however, had plenty of time to think about their conversations.

"She knows something about the legends," he muttered. There had to be truth to it. Why else would she be so protective of a myth?

Maybe he could get her to tell him about it. Maybe. He was running low on toothpaste, so he wasn't sure how charming he could be without clean teeth, if she took too long to come back. If she came back.

Holding the fishing rod between his knees, he pulled his t-shirt off, pulling a tail of it through is belt loop to tie it in place, ran his hands through his hair to free it of tangles and resumed the fishing.

Eventually he caught a few good-sized fish, saw the mystery birds a couple of times and was disappointed there was no Kymri, again. Gathering up his things, he headed back to camp, following the foot path he'd tracked Kymri with.

He was surprised with the sight of her when he emerged from the woods. Looking over his encampment, she stood by his equipment boxes, peering into the top one. He had a perfect view of her ass. His hands itched to slide up her hips and grip her narrow waist.

"Welcome back, Kymri."

She spun around at the sound of his voice, her eyes widened, hands behind her back, which fortunately for him pushed her chest out, stretching the cotton across her generous breasts.

"Oh, hello Jori."

"What are you doing over there?" he set the fish and rod aside, approaching her.

She shrugged, her gaze sweeping him from head to toe, lingering on his bare chest. "What do your markings mean?" she said after a moment.

Glancing down, he realized she meant his tattoos.

She stepped forward to get a closer look, lips parted. "Very intricate and colorful."

She smelled amazing.

"Just some artwork my mother did when I was a kid, and I had it made into tattoos."

"There is something familiar about the designs." Her eyes drifted across his chest. "Who are Jonathan and Elora?"

He glanced down at the entwined names, "My parents."

"It's lovely. I knew an Elora, once—a long time ago." One of her hands reached out, stopping just inches shy of his skin, "May I?"

"Sure." His pulse tripped.

Her fingers tentatively slid over his skin following the lines.

His breath stilled at the electric sensation traveling along her touch. The hairs rose on his arms along with immediate arousal.

"What were you doing over by the cases?" he asked, his voice growing husky.

"Nothing," she said after a moment.

"What's in your hand behind your back?"

Her head jerked up; eyes wide. She was so close to him.

As he looked down into her face, he just wanted to kiss her parted lips. He leaned over her and he could feel the electricity crackle between them. Reaching around, he slid his hand down her arm to her hand as he stared at her mouth.

She seemed as mesmerized as he almost was. His fingers curled around hers and felt the smooth edge of something in her hand.

His lips brushed hers. Barely a breath. He wanted more, yet held back.

It was enough to pull the objects from her hand. They were the batteries from his devices.

Stepping away from her he said, "What are you doing with these?"

She blinked at him, reality returning, and she saw the batteries she'd had clenched in her fist now in his hand. Straightening her shoulders, her chin inched up. The soft lips he'd kissed a moment before compressed into a hard line. She lunged for him, her breasts colliding with solid muscle of his chest when he twisted, throwing his hand up where she couldn't reach it.

He repeated his question.

She pulled her knife and stepped back, placing her feet for better balance. "Don't make me hurt you," she said.

Jori had traveled long and far enough to know that anyone who carried a weapon, likely knew how to use it. "Just tell me what you want with the batteries from my equipment."

Her fierce scowl deepened, "I will protect my people any way I have to. I don't want to have to kill you, but I will."

"You'd kill me over camera batteries?"

Her nod was sharp, and she shifted the knife in her hand, drawing his attention.

Was his life worth the batteries? The batteries meant his ability to record. If he couldn't record anything the entire excursion was a waste of time and resources.

He stared at her. And it was then he knew, absolutely, there was something here. No one would react the way she was if there weren't.

His mother's words drifted back to him—*there's always another way to achieve a goal*.

Lowering his hand, he held it out to her, open palm up.

Her eyes flicked between his hand and his face then snatched and threw them as hard as she could into the ocean.

He cringed, knowing what that would do to the immediate environment.

Kymri's posture relaxed, then she sheathed her knife.

Jori walked over the to the equipment boxes, looking in each one. At least she hadn't damaged the units themselves. Later he'd move the memory cards into sealed cases and slip them under the foam casing.

He wouldn't tell her she hadn't taken all of the batteries, there were spares still in the plane.

Threat removed, her demeanor changed. "Tell me more of yourself and where you come from," she said, as though there hadn't been a sharp blade between them moments before.

"Well, uh… What do you want to know?"

She thought a moment for a specific question, "Where is your home?"

"I have a condo in Philly, for now, and a cottage up at Lac L'Achigan in Canada, but I don't spend much time at either."

"You don't have a regular home?"

He shrugged, "Haven't really found the right place that felt like a home. I'm used to being on the move."

"I couldn't imagine that."

So, she clearly was deeply rooted. No wonder she was willing to cut him to defend it from what she thought was some kind of a threat.

"Tell me something of your home."

Her gaze shot to his face, studying him. "It is a good place to live. We work hard to keep it going." She considered him again, "What is your role?"

"My role? What I do for work?"

She nodded.

"As I said before, I'm a documenter. I travel the world visiting new and unusual places, recording each excursion. With the material I gather I make documentaries for people to watch and publish companion books with the photos and essays."

"That doesn't sound very difficult or practical."

"That's what my father says." He was a little stung to hear her opinion on the matter.

"It's important to you?"

He nodded, lacing his hands together.

"Well then, I suppose that's what matters, then?" Her hand slid over his.

He looked up into her apologetic expression. She squeezed his hand and let go.

"What of you?"

"I'm a guardian."

"I should have figured that out." He grinned.

She smiled and her whole face changed. It was such a genuine smile. His heart flipped over and his breath went elsewhere.

She looked softer and almost impish when she wasn't stern and scowling.

His fingers twitched, wanting to touch her skin and her wild hair.

Something shifted between them. Her hand slid over his again and her eyes were on his mouth.

He leaned in. He wanted to kiss her for real this time.

Kymri's hand slid over Jori's, enjoying the feel of the strong muscle beneath the tanned and tattooed skin. Her eyes fixed on his full lips and she wondered if his beard would be soft.

He leaned toward her and her breath stalled.

Earlier she'd been so distracted when his lips had brushed across hers, and it had caught her by surprise.

Now, she was attentive. Waiting.

She watched his face inch closer, his eyes on her mouth. Her tongue darted out in anticipation and he closed the distance.

Eyes closed, she reveled in the sensation of his soft lips moving over hers and his facial hair on her skin. Soft and scratchy all at once.

After a moment, his tongue tested her lips. Desire shot down through to her belly. Her lips opened to him; her hands slid up his forearms. He closed the gap between them, pulling her against him, leaving no doubt about his reciprocated desire for her. She groaned as he deepened the kiss and her hands had somehow worked their way up into his hair. One of his large hands cupped her face so she couldn't escape, the other spanned the small of her back, keeping her pressed against him.

He eventually broke the kiss, resting his forehead on hers as they caught their breath, his rough thumb stroked the delicate flesh between her lower lip and her chin.

"You're so beautiful," he breathed so that she barely heard him.

The sounds of the ocean crashing on the beach around them matched the rushing of her pulse.

"Stay with me."

Kymri leaned back enough to search his face. It was full of desire and familiar longing. She drew in a deep breath, scenting his musk, letting it infuse her so that it would never leave her memory.

She nodded, "For a little while."

Jori lowered his head to touch her lips again and her chest filled with the sweetness of it. Her fingers slid along his jaw and he caught her hand, kissing her fingertips once he released her lips, keeping their hands entwined as he pulled her toward the beach, "Let's walk a bit. Talk."

She smiled as shyness suddenly swept through her. She felt as ridiculously giddy as a developing youngling.

They walked the beach until the light dimmed. There was less talking than intended, as they needed to stop every now and then to kiss again.

It was at some point during this time that they became two very different people from who they were in their separate worlds. The bond hooked, sinking its barb with that first kiss, then began to thread around them.

They did chat about the beach, fish, the island and the ocean. The state of Jori's plane, and his frustration and inability to get his equipment working to call for help.

"I will see if I can find help for you, but I can't promise anything."

"Fair enough," he said. They had reached the camp and it was growing dark. He retrieved his shirt and pulled it over his head.

They both stared at the small tent.

"Jori, I can't take you back with me, at least not yet." She turned to face him.

"Of course," he said, his voice wasn't as easy as it had been moments before.

She didn't give him an explanation, nor did he ask for one.

He didn't ask for her to stay or return.

Instead, he stared into her eyes so that she could see the flecks of color in his irises even in the fading light, and brought his hands up over her shoulders, slid them up her neck—sending shivers through her body—to cup her face. Then very, very deliberately let his gaze smolder as he dropped his focus to her lips, stretching out the seconds until he decided he was ready to taste her again.

Her insides felt as though she'd done barrel rolls through descending altitude.

By the time he was done with her she had nearly decided his small tent was the perfect place for their first mating.

When she started to sink into him, he eased the kiss and backed away, releasing her face.

She blinked, then remembered to breathe.

"It's getting dark." She had to finish her patrol and report back. "I have to go," she said and turned to walk back through the woods on weak legs.

Chapter 6

J ori watched her go, hips swaying as she climbed the rise through the trees.

He seriously questioned the sanity of letting her go.

He was painfully engorged and all he could think about were her lips and the feel of her body pressed to his. He'd developed fantasies of devouring her body and pounding her till she screamed with ecstasy days ago. Several rolled through his brain, making him throb with a hair trigger.

He stripped down, leaving his clothes in the middle of his camp where he dropped them and went straight into the warm sea water.

The waves lapped at him until the water was above his waist. His hands slid over his cock and began to work it. Images of Kymri in various positions, sighing and moaning, rolled through his mind. Biting her and licking her lips, his lips, his flesh, her mouth encasing his cock.

Lying on her back, thighs wide, while he licked every inch of her. Jori lying on his back while she rode him, grinding, her breasts heavy, her nipples taut.

Kymri bent over while his hands gripped her round hips as he pounded into her.

He groaned her name as he came, head thrown back.

When the orgasm subsided and he opened his eyes to the vast sky, a long-tailed bird flew past high overhead.

He stood breathless for several moments, staring at the brightening constellation of the dragon.

Kymri adjusted the angle of her wings as she glided over the city toward the patrol tower's platform. The image of watching Jori alone in the sea after she left him was hovering in her mind, distracting her from focusing on her duty. He was inhibiting her ability to do her job properly. Closing her eyes and clearing her mind of the tumbling erotic desires, she set herself right and finished her patrol, spiraling her flight pattern back toward the core of the dragon territory.

Below her, women worked in their gardens and bustled along narrow paths between patchwork properties. The central marketplace was so alive that she could smell the wares and hear the calls and hagglers from her height. She loved the view of her city from this vantage point, where everything looked as though it were in miniature. She glanced at the queen's tower as she banked and turned toward the landing platform.

She could see her mother watching her come into land. Her jaw clenched and the ease and budding happiness that had been creeping into her dissipated with a little fizzle.

As soon as Kymri landed, Kolina pounced, "Where have you been?"

Irritation rumbled in Kymri's chest before she shifted into human form. "Doing my job," she snapped, bypassing her parent to retrieve her robe from the change room.

"You're late."

"Yes I am. And?"

"You're never late."

"Right."

"I'm told there's an intruder on an outer island."

Kymri paused, fastening the buttons on her robe. "There is."

"Why haven't you eliminated them?"

"I was assessing threat level."

"Your job is to keep everyone out."

"I know my job. Why are you here instead of doing yours?"

"I'm also told you've been fraternizing with the intruder instead of getting rid of him." Kolina's gaze was hyper focused on her daughter's face.

"I told you I was assessing whether or not he was a threat."

Suspicion suddenly glimmered in Kolina's eyes; her posture eased back as she considered her daughter anew. "He." Kolina's nostrils flared, scenting Kymri.

Kymri ignored it. "He's stranded."

"Has council been notified?"

"The situation is documented in our reports, we haven't reached the point in our schedule to relay them to the counsel yet."

"Schedules are overridden when there is a threat," Kolina reminded her.

"He isn't a threat."

"And you just know this because?"

"As you said, I've been fraternizing with him."

"Have you mated with him yet?"

Kymri blinked at the sudden turn of subject. "No," she said through clenched teeth.

"Do it and get rid of him."

"Why would you think I'd mate with him?"

"I can smell him on you, you've clearly been in considerable contact beyond an assessment," Kolina said. "And it's my understanding you've been uncharacteristically distracted and moody, risking your ability to do your work."

Kymri's hackles went up, "Who?"

Kolina's lips compressed.

"You have someone spying on me?"

Her mother maintained her silence, and her anger bubbled.

"Do your schemes never stop? What did you do to me? Did you put a tincture in my food or drug me in some other way to try to get me to do what you want?"

Kolina's brow went up, curiosity in her eyes, "What makes you think I would do such a thing?" she said with exaggerated innocence.

"Because I know you'll do whatever it takes to get what you want, and you've been riding my scales to mate and have young."

Kolina watched Kymri carefully.

Kymri's sudden flare of anger and pent up frustrations rippled through her body.

"You're not even denying it."

Kolina's expression shifted, "You're experiencing a heat."

"What did you do to me?"

"Nothing, Kymri. You need to mate."

"I won't give you the satisfaction."

Kolina's brows shot up at the ridiculousness of the comment, "Kymri, you're not behaving like yourself. If you don't mate, you will jeopardize everything you value."

Kymri recognized it as soon as it passed her lips. She refused to let Kolina manipulate her. She ignored the glimmer of compassion in her mother's eyes. Fighting for reason, she turned and left her mother. Kolina didn't stop her.

She didn't go to her office, as was expected, to fill out the report needed to complete her shift, instead she headed out to look for Marli to vent to.

Unable to find her, she went to her room to try to find her self-control. This was foreign to her.

The haze of frustration slid over her. She felt as though she were losing her mind. Locking her door, she unbuttoned her robe and hung it on a nearby hook before going to bathe, hoping the process would calm her as it usually did.

Whatever this was, it wasn't simply desire. She'd mated before, always careful to not conceive, and while it was enjoyable, it was just an enjoyable activity with a man. There were very few men on the island at any given time. Almost none at all. The queen didn't want them here.

Would Jori want to stay for her? She knew she wouldn't want to leave, even if she did want him with her, the pressure for him to go would be intense for both of them.

Did she want him that much? How could she possibly know that already? The little tickle at the back of her mind hinted otherwise.

Shoving her face under the flow of the water sprinkling over her to drown the budding thought, she switched topics on the same subject; remembering the feel of his kiss and his body. He clearly desired her, the length and hardness of his male organ was obvious. She sighed, reaching for the soap and lathering her hair and body. He'd bathed in the ocean. Her soapy hands slid over her peaked nipples, sending a thrum of desire straight down to the apex of her thighs, making her whole body jerk. She was too tense. With water flowing over her, one hand worked her breasts while the other slid into herself, moving her fingers through her own heat and wetness. Imagining they were his strong fingers and lips on her, she came with a shudder, allowing the flowing water to wash away the tension.

It wasn't enough, but it was enough for now. Stemming the water, she reached for a towel to wrap around herself and moved to the small vanity in her room. She thought about her mother's words as she pulled a brush through her hair.

Heat.

She'd suspected as much from what she'd been able to find in the archive on dragon anatomy. It didn't happen to everyone— then most dragonesses had their young long before the point she was in her life now. In reality it was rare and seemed most common for metal dragons. Physicians and philosophers had theories without anything solidly clinical to explain it. Astrologers said it was a cosmic tie to the dragon stars and the coming of the comet that begat the mutation of their particular dragon species.

Kymri didn't know what to think of any of it. It seemed to be happening, and happening to her. Now.

She thought it had more to do with Jori in some way. It wasn't a factor until he appeared within their boundaries. She couldn't be sure what was causing it, only that he affected its intensity. Jori muddled her ability to think straight.

Would the problem go away if she just bedded him? She didn't have to conceive, no matter what her mother expected of her. Mate with him, then see him on his way. Maybe. She sighed. It was just mating; it wasn't a big deal.

It wasn't as though other men hadn't been to the city, they just were expected to go back to where they came from.

So, what was she afraid of?

Tossing her brush on the vanity, she rifled through the collection of brightly colored nail polish.

She could bring him to the city. Just for a little while.

Then he'd learn their secret, which he'd come all this way to expose to the world.

Would he change his mind? Could she trust him?

She picked the hot pink.

Did she have to? She'd destroyed his batteries, and the equipment wasn't functioning properly inside their magnetic field. Maybe it was a moot point.

The varnish remover stung her nose as the old color worked into the cotton.

Yes, she could just bed him and send him home.

Her heart twisted a little as an image of his charming smile popped into her mind.

She had her duty and he didn't belong here.

He'd said he didn't really belong anywhere.

The brush flicked the hot pink color onto her nails with quick practiced strokes.

That didn't sit well with her.

Lips pursed, her breath was gentle across the fresh paint.

That was better.

Dressing, mind settled, she returned to the patrol office to complete her report. It was almost time to go to the council.

Almost.

Chapter 7

There was little to do on the island.

Jori had already jogged the perimeter, collected fresh water and coconuts.

His notebook had gone from pages of notes to attempts at sketching Kymri. His talent wasn't enough to do her justice.

Wisps of cloud slid over the island and the horizon was shrouded in a haze.

Gathering up his sleeping bag and pillow, he moved it to the plane. He'd already rearranged the cases and equipment out of boredom. The space was adequate to keep him dry while he slept.

He blew out a breath, longing for a proper bed and shower. He was tired of the grit of sand and sea salt. His skin never felt smoother, but the stuff got everywhere.

Hands on hips, he surveyed the monotonous view of his camp. Wreck, fire pit and chairs, palm forest, beach and sea. And sky. Plenty of that too.

Dropping his head back, he peered into the endless blue, masked here and there by cloud wisps and a long-tailed bird high above.

He still had no idea what breed it was. That was the first thing he'd do when he got home - after a long hot shower.

If. If he got home.

What was taking so long for Kymri's people to help a guy out?

Did they know he existed? They must.

A cold chill swept through him.

What if they didn't?

What if she was keeping his presence a secret for some crazy reason?

"Nah... She's not crazy." There was a good reason for his continued stay here.

Right?

How long *had* he been here? *Just a few days.*

They have to decide if you're a threat, he reminded himself.

He recalled some of the villages he and his mother had visited in his youth. Some places welcomed visitors. Others, well, other villages required his mother's solid negotiation skills.

This was probably one of those instances.

The photo of his mother from his control panel had been lost during the crash. He'd hoped to magically find it lodged somewhere in the plane. Despite several attempts to find it, he hadn't.

God, he missed her.

"I know, I know. Be patient."

He stripped off his shirt, tossing it into the open door of the plane.

Jori hated waiting, may as well go for another run to kill the time. He'd be triathlon ready by the time rescue came with all the running, swimming and palm tree climbing lately.

This trip wasn't supposed to have gone like this.

It should have been an easy flight with smooth skies, friendly villagers, and beautiful photos for his book. Something tangible made from the stories his mother told him over and over throughout his childhood. He had created the persona of a legend hunter for his online show, adventuring to exotic places, meeting cool folks and making lifelong memories. This trip was supposed to be that, dedicated to his mom.

She disappeared. He assumed she was dead. He had to. Or else, why wouldn't she have ever come back?

He swallowed hard, picking up speed.

She wouldn't have just left him and his dad. She wouldn't.

One day she told him she had to take a trip to the Bahamas.

The next day his world fell apart.

The incredible relationship he had with his father withered.

At thirteen, he swallowed his grief.

They didn't speak of her. He'd tried, but gotten nowhere. His father always changed the subject.

So, he locked it away and got on with living.

His father got on with existing.

Jori was determined not to fade like that. He was going to make something of her memory.

After a time, he no longer noticed the sorrow in his father's eyes. He went his own way. Like his mother always did. He looked on his father's life as a small confined world, existing on his little campus, surrounded by transient students and emotionally distant colleagues.

He hated that place. He couldn't breathe from the time he set foot on campus till he could escape again. The regimented life scraped at his psyche. Confinement, authority, suffocation.

He drew air deeper into his lungs, his feet pounded the hot sand.

"Fuck."

He needed something to do.

There was too much fucking time to think.

Too much time alone.

Disappointment swept through Kymri. Jori wasn't in his camp. She sighed; he couldn't be far. The island was small. She just hoped he hadn't seen her land. Wandering through the beach space he'd made his own, she saw the bedroll was moved into the body of his plane.

Peaking inside, she noticed the book abandoned on the fabric. Picking it up, she leafed through pages and pages of dense notes in tight, neat handwriting, broken with small sketches here and there.

She recognized the shape of a dragon in flight, drawn in miniature. So, he had seen the patrols.

Then there was a sketch of the sky and several constellations.

She smiled at pages of palm trees, the plane and campfire.

Her throat clamped shut as she turned the page.

Sketches of herself. In profile, different angles, focused aspects of her face. The likeness was remarkable. Right down to the placement of her freckles.

The book snapped shut.

Of course, he'd drawn her. He'd already exhausted the other subjects in his vicinity.

It was nothing.

She cracked it open again. She looked awfully sultry in one of the portraits.

Her skin flushed.

She tossed it back on the bedroll and noticed the discarded shirt.

It was faded from the intense sun and sea salt.

She picked it up, bringing it to her nose.

It smelled of sunshine, ocean and him.

Inhaling deeper, her dragon growled, eyes glazing over.

Heat flared through her body from her molten core like a flash of quicksilver.

Her body shook as she exhaled, struggling to control the sudden surge of raw sexual instinct.

Resisting the urge to rub her face on the fabric, she slowly put it beside the book and backed away drawing deep breaths.

Control.

She had to cool down.

Turning toward the ocean, Kymri walked into the water without bothering to remove her clothing.

Dragon goddess! She had never experienced anything like *that* before.

Soothing water flowed around her, easing the flare.

She sighed, closing her eyes, floating.

She opened her eyes at the sound of panting.

Jori ran into her line of view, his deeply tanned skin glistened over flexing muscles.

Her dragon noticed.

Kymri prayed his scent wouldn't carry. She swallowed hard, trying to decide what to do; alert him to her presence or maintain her silence and watch?

Despite the distance, he was crystal clear. Every line of muscle. Lean arms, taut abs, strong back. His shorts rode low on his hips.

Her tongue smoothed over her lip, wondering what he tasted like.

He unwound the elastic holding the hair from his face, letting it tumble lose as he turned toward the ocean and froze.

"Kymri?"

She hadn't realized she was moving toward him until his gaze swept down her body. She could feel the thin cotton plastered to her skin.

His eyes lingered on her breasts, sweeping lower.

"*Christ*," he muttered, dragging his eyes back to her face.

She reached for him.

He stared at her parted lips as she moved into him, pressing her ocean cooled body to his. Hands twining around his neck, she pulled his face down to hers and devoured his mouth.

His tongue swept into her mouth as his arms crushed her against him.

She couldn't get enough, rubbing her hips against his.

He broke the kiss, "Kymri, what's going on here?" He was still panting. She wasn't sure if it was from the run or their kissing.

"I-I just wanted to be here with you," she whispered, her fingers tangling in his hair.

"I'm sweaty."

"I know."

He grinned down at her and she melted.

The flare was building again. "I need you."

His brow lifted.

Her hands slid down his torso to the waist of his shorts.

He stopped breathing as her fingers made contact with the hard steel of his member.

Her dragon purred. Her vision glazed and she closed her eyes to let it pass, her fist tightening around him.

He pressed into her hand; his mouth came down over hers again with a growl.

Releasing him, she struggled to push the restricting shorts off his hips.

He caught her hands. "Whoa, slow down, love," he exhaled with a shudder, eyes closed. He drew a breath, set his shoulders and leveled his gaze on her face, seeming to drink her in. "Are you sure?"

"Damned sure," she said, trying to free her hands so they could roam over him. Her heart fluttered when he smiled again. It was crooked and mischievous.

"Give me just a minute. Just a minute, I promise," he said when she opened her mouth to protest.

He kissed her, releasing her hands, and ran into the surf.

Kymri burned while she watched him bathe in the sea. Without thought, she was walking back into the water to join him.

He laughed. Instead of opening his arms to her, he scooped her up and carried her back toward the beach, setting her down beside the open door of the plane. Reaching in, he grabbed the book and shirt and tossed them onto the pilot seat, then turned his attention to Kymri. Her hands were on him already.

Eyes on her breasts, visible through the cotton shirt, his hands were warm when they eased over her hips, sliding up her waist, dragging the shirt up over her head. His lips met hers, tongues testing each other, then his mouth and hands were on her breasts.

She groaned.

The sensations of his warm, moist mouth, slick tongue, strong hands and soft-scratchy beard across her sensitive flesh stoked the blaze in her.

His hands slid back to her hips, kissing his way lower over her ribs and belly.

She shivered.

His fingers hooked into the waistband of her pants, dragging them down, kissing her skin as it was exposed. He paused at the apex of her thighs, drew a deep breath, kissed each thigh, and freed her feet of the fabric, then guided her to sit on the bedroll. He used her abandoned pants to wipe the sand from her feet and draped her clothing over the ledge of the open window.

He did the same with his shorts.

She stared at his naked body, admiring the sight of him.

He was ready for her.

She scooted back to make room for him. He reached for her, drawing her back where she was and settled between her thighs, lips returning to her belly.

His eyes twinkled when he looked at her face, lips quirked as he gently moved her leg so that her inner knee rested on his shoulder.

Watching him through a haze of desire, her body smoldered as he lowered his head to kiss her thigh, so close to her core. His tongue tasted her wetness and she fell back onto her elbows with a groan.

His tongue, dear dragongoddess, his tongue licked and delved, gentle then insistent, lips suckling and nipping over and over again.

Eyes closed; her world went white, light blazing behind her eyelids. His mouth didn't stop until her shudders did.

With a final kiss on her thigh, he looked up at her, his face taut with desire.

He stood, intending to crawl in beside her, but when his erection wavered in front of her, she growled and grabbed him.

Startled, he didn't move.

His eyes were heavy as he looked down at her gripping him. She licked her lips and took him into her mouth, working him as he had her. His head fell back, fingers sliding through her hair, gentle.

"Stop," he gasped after a few moments.

Releasing him, she smiled and moved back onto the bedroll to make room for him. He took her place and swept her into his arms so that she straddled him, his face level with her breasts.

He planted his mouth on a nipple. She gasped as he slid his fingers along her hyper-sensitive wet flesh.

Catching his face between her hands, she stared into his eyes, kissing him as deeply as she could, mingling her tongue with his, then broke away to look at him again.

Thick brows, long lashes, eyes that sparkled when he looked at her. Strong nose and full lips framed by his trimmed beard. The hair that was normally tied up fell around his shoulders now, damp with sea water.

She memorized him, imprinting.

He seemed to be doing the same. His hand rose to stroke her jaw.

Slowly, she lowered her hips, impaling herself on him.

He drew in a shuddered breath as she exhaled a shuddered breath.

Finally, united.

They drank in each other's faces, just breathing.

She wanted to stay as they were forever.

At the same time, her hips were compelled to move. Her muscles held every inch of his hard flesh tight.

He leaned in to lick her throat. Her head fell back to expose more of it to his mouth, reveling in the sensation as she rocked her hips.

Teeth nipped her fevered skin. Her fingers dug into his shoulders, his fingers dug into her hips, guiding her so she plunged down on him, harder, faster, nipples grazing his chest.

His left arm slid around her hips locking her in place, his right stroked up her back to grip the base of her neck, driving her down.

"Jori!"

She exploded again, gripping him so tight she thought she was going to die. Through the blinding haze, she was acutely aware of him expanding and surging inside of her.

He exhaled on a long breath, his forehead pressed to her chest.

He looked up into her face, lids heavy, then pulled her down to kiss him. He drew his long legs up into the plane and shifted them so they could lay back on the bedroll, Kymri still atop him. Jori still inside her.

They rested for a short while before the exploration of each other's bodies began in earnest.

It was very late by the time Kymri flew back to the guard tower platform. She went straight to her office to make her report ready to present to the council.

She couldn't leave him on the beach anymore.

Her fingers drummed the desktop. The hot pink of her nails drew her attention to the memory of him admiring the color and kissing each finger, his tongue slipping over the sensitive pads of her fingertips.

What do I do?

She wanted to keep him.

He needed to get home.

He wouldn't be allowed to stay.

And she had her duty to protect her queen and her people.

Invaders

S tenlen soared over the open ocean, his subordinates off either wingtip.

The human's last broadcast had stated he was headed toward these coordinates.

There was something here.

The scent in the air signaled a change in magnetic energy. He dipped through several layers of cloud, banking and rolling to break the monotony of the endless ocean and sky. It helped a little. He'd rather be flying over the mountain ranges and forests back home.

An unfamiliar scent drifted past his nostrils, triggering the urge to hunt.

Female, and nearby.

He followed it, his companions flying close behind trailing in his wake, moving almost as a unit.

He snarled; he could taste her in the air, they were fucking close!

He couldn't believe it.

The human had let them to the dragonesses.

He could taste her.

It was a thin stream of scent in the air. Distinctive. Keeping his nostrils aligned with the drifting scent, he followed it further and further to the east, pulling him along like a bull ring in his nose. He was latched on and was not going to let it go.

They'd waited far too long to find their lair.

Maybe there was only one dragon—like the last time they managed to trap one?

No, where there was one, there were more. They stayed glued together like hens, and he would swallow them all up.

Excitement rippled through him.

He heard the growls coming from behind him. They had scented her too, edging them forward, the instinct to pursue driving at them.

The scent grew stronger, it wouldn't be long.

He realized they were traveling in an arc, no matter, they'd follow it. Around and around, it pulled them in a massive spiral, an orbit.

He could feel it in his scales and ridges.

They were circling something important. The queen? Would they be so lucky?

He snuffed and angled his wings in tighter then signaled his wing men to fan out.

She was close...

A small dark form in the distance appeared and he knew it wasn't a bird. Good.

So fucking good.

He could barely contain the rush.

How long had it been since they'd had females? Real females, not the weak human ones. Genuine dragon females that could take a real dragon man.

They couldn't hide from them anymore. It was time for them to return to accept their places under the guidance of male dragons. Reunite the sexes of the species.

Up ahead, the little dragoness veered away from the trajectory she'd originally been flying in.

She must have sighted or sensed them.

She was trying to lead them away from her treasure island.

Go for the island, or go for her?

He made the decision to pursue her. They could make her talk without them having to spend wasted hours flying over the ocean. She could tell them exactly where the rest of them were.

Just a little patience. And a little intimidation — but only if she made it necessary.

He growled and his wingmen banked as they all three drove forward.

They'd drive her down into the ocean if they had to. They wouldn't be leaving this region without her. She was too valuable.

Stenlen's chest thumped with adrenaline, his lips pulling back over his teeth as they drove her on.

After a while, her speed lagged, her altitude dipped, and she changed directions to coast on the wind current.

She was almost spent.

The smell of land washed over him.

She was going for the islands. It didn't matter.

They weren't going to let her escape them.

A dark line rose out of the distance, bisecting the sea and sky and the small form in the air dipped and dove for the water.

He grinned.

He had her scent; he would soon have her taste too.

As soon as they were within human sight distance, he drove the trio down into the water sliding through the ocean toward the islands.

He continued swimming once the momentum began to drag, then surfaced enough to draw breath.

In the distance, he could make out the crescent of sandy beach dotted with people.

While in the water, he couldn't tell if she kept going straight or if she broke away and veered off in one direction or another.

His men broke away to pursue each option as he continued forward toward the populated beach. Once he reached the land shelf he shifted into human form, swimming forward until he blended with the humans.

He slowed his pace only stopping when he reached waist height in the water. He was bare, as would she be.

Would she risk emerging naked?

He scanned the space trying to pick her out of the crowded beach and laughed.

It was a hedonistic resort.

Striding forward, his eyes scanned the people, trying to pick her out, ignoring the appreciative glances the human women were training on him.

While their shapes were pleasing, he was fully focused on finding his dragon woman.

His nostrils flared, hoping to pick up residual scents of her despite her human form.

He couldn't smell her anymore.

He stopped to scan again.

Had she come this way? He couldn't be sure, as soon as they shifted to human form, the scent was masked, and the trail went thin.

Dammit.

There were too many here. His head swung from side to side, trying to hone in on the right woman, but there were none alone. They were in pairs, groups or with men.

"Hey there, luv, want to join us for a drink?"

His head jerked toward the voice. A bottle blond eyed him up, taking her time. Her gaze trailed and lingered over his groin before flicking up to his face.

Would she be so bold to confront him directly?

The woman stood before him, barbells through her nipples and a diamond in the dimple of her belly button, a thin tattoo spiraled up her ankle. She had several friends looking on with interest.

"Come on, have some fun," she said, shifting her body in invitation toward the small group. There were a couple of guys with them.

"Some other time." He winked at her and turned toward the path that led back to the resort.

Striding up the incline, he drew a deep breath, nostrils wide. Only ripe human and sunscreen lotion and alcohol.

Fuck.

He hoped Clive and Merwin were able to track her.

He wandered through the complex like he was a resident, smiling at random women that showed interest in him, and even a few good-looking men. He continued wandering, determined to find her.

By the time he wandered back out to the beach, his men were there waiting for him, acting like locals.

As soon as they sighted him, they both gave a shake of their heads.

Damn.

She had to have come this way, if they hadn't found her, then she was here somewhere.

But if she wasn't?

He ran a hand through his wet hair.

Back to the skies to retrace where they'd originally picked up her scent.

They were too close not to follow up. He had a job to do and he wasn't going to let his king down.

They at least knew roughly where she'd come from.

Marli held her breath until her chest burned, threatening to suck sea water into her lungs.

Watching from the seabed, shielded by the sea shelf, the large shape drifted overhead, blocking out the sun.

Dear dragoness, he was huge.

How long had it been since she saw a male dragon? She'd forgotten how big they were.

Had she seen three of them pursuing her? There was only one here.

The other two must have gone around to flank her.

As soon as his large mass drifted far enough away, she kicked up to the surface, greedily sucking air into her lungs, watching him swim toward the beach, head turning, clearly looking for her.

She kept her distance in case he turned around. He didn't. He was focused on the people ahead of them. She swam to the left, toward a group playing a game with a floating ball, intending to mix with them, trailing him, moving from group to group, blending. She watched the female humans approach him, inviting, disappointed.

His body was toned and attractive, water trailing down his body.

He was dangerous, not just to her, but to her queen and her heirs.

There were far more important things to focus on than lust.

She worked her way forward, careful not to draw too much attention as she plucked a bottle of lotion to rub onto her skin, then an abandoned drink, letting it splash on herself to mask her scent, stumbling in the sand from group to group moving closer until he disappeared into the building complex. She waited by the beach for him to either return or disappear completely.

Her patience paid off as he reappeared, walking toward her.

Her gaze slipped along the front of him. Nice.

She watched his face, still searching, then head toward two men.

Breath held, timing her movements so that she walked past them with a small group of women heading up to the resort.

"Nothing, she's gone," he said.

Where his features were sharp, the other two were blunt and bland.

"Maybe she's heading back, and we can pick up her trail again."

"I don't think so, - it doesn't matter. She was circling something—it has to be her tribe."

"We're close."

"Come on, have some fun now, we'll head out again soon."

"If she warns them, we won't be able to get close."

"Doesn't matter, we can pick off their patrols and bring them back for the stable."

Marli tripped, spilling the drink, making a show of swiping the liquor off her arm and chest, drawing his eyes.

Glancing up, seeing his attention on her, she winked and tipped her head, "Shame to waste good liquor." She pouted.

His gaze slid down her form, he started to move forward. She glanced up toward the resort and made like she saw someone she knew, waving. She threw him a smile and trotted up the sand maintaining proximity to the group of women.

Shit.

What the hell was she going to do now? If she flew back, they'd catch her scent and just follow her.

If she didn't, the island would be ignorant of their coming.

Marli needed to get help, and she prayed she would be in time.

Chapter 8

K ymri walked out of the council room, growls rumbling in her chest.

She'd presented the reports showing sparse activity in the region. Red's pirate ship had been spotted before the storm, but otherwise was absent from the boundary region. The cruise ships were maintaining their sail routes parallel to their borders staying well outside the periphery, as were air vehicles. The US military were still sending out their planes, and they too were respecting the magnetic boundary, having learned the expensive lesson of losing their planes—to both navigation failure and dragon deflection—when they didn't.

The only trespasser was Jori, who'd drifted into their territory on his little plane. They'd kept an eye on him regularly, documenting visible activities and she had gone to assess him herself.

The queen had been on the throne, in its position on the dais behind the gathered Council. Her personal guard surrounded her.

Kymri's mother was at the queen's side.

The questions began. Why did you push his plane to safety rather than eliminate him immediately? Why didn't you leave him to his fate on the ocean, he may have drifted out again on his own?

"Council, it's been many, many years since we've had a drifter. And despite the sensitivity around the queen's safety since the last attack we defended against, I thought it prudent not to unnecessarily destroy a citizen of our neighboring nation. For the sake of peace, we would expect that had one of our citizens drifted into their territory they would not be destroyed."

"No, they'd lock her up indefinitely." One of the councillors muttered.

"That may be, in current conditions, Madam Councillor, but not all of their regimes have been so barbaric. And in light of the hard work that Queen and Council have done to form political bonds, I thought it best to maintain a stance of neighborly compassion until the situation had been thoroughly assessed."

"And now that you've had personal contact, what have you assessed the threat level to be, Kymri Steelscale?"

"As my reports state, the drifter is a lone male of prime age from the continent. His navigation and communication equipment failed when he passed through the barrier and became stranded. He carries recording and documentation equipment for his travels."

"What is the subject of his documentation?"

"Us."

Murmurs rippled through the gathered dragons.

"He and his equipment need to be destroyed."

There were several other outbursts before Madam Councillor gained control of the gathering. "Continue your report, guardian commander." Her voice had gone hard, signaling Kymri's fragile standing.

"The equipment is non-functional and the batteries that power them have been destroyed."

"She should have destroyed all of it," another councillor said.

"I did not see the point in destroying the man's livelihood altogether, the intention was to send him on his way back to the continent."

"Guardian, why did you not take care of this threat at any point over the last days of the drifter's presence?"

Kymri opened her mouth to speak, but she was cut off before she could answer.

"Because she's gone into heat and her judgment should be questioned."

Kymri's heart sank as her head turned toward the familiar voice.

Zayli.

The murmurs rose among the gathered again.

Kymri's gaze found her mother, who'd blanched.

She didn't think this was part of her mother's schemes. Her cousin had just betrayed her. She then looked to her queen, who returned her attention with mild curiosity.

The councillors were a different matter.

Some looked on her with pity, some with disgust, some smiled as they looked down on her.

"Madam Councillor, in light of this information, any assessment Guardian Commander Kymri Steelscale provides is untrustworthy, especially since the drifter is male. She should be relieved of duty and he should be destroyed."

Panic ripped through Kymri and she fought hard to suppress the growl that threatened to erupt in the council chamber. She trembled from the self-control required to stay her involuntary defensive shift into her dragon form at the thought of Jori's death.

"He can't be destroyed," she said, her voice strained with the effort of controlling herself. "The mating bond is threading." The words flew out of her mouth and she wasn't sure they were truth until the turmoil inside her calmed once they were said.

She had just sealed both their fates, and her position as guardian commander might still be lost to her.

The Council had a brief recess before Madam Councillor conferred with the queen.

The decision was passed to retrieve Jori and his equipment from the island; they would do their own investigation.

Her chest was tight as she reached her private quarters. She paced the room, stripping off her formal council robes.

She was as agitated over the realization that the bond was indeed in process as she was about the threat to Jori. And then there was the betrayal of Zayli. She changed her clothes and prepared for the retrieval, then descended to meet with the expedition team.

Madam Councillor and Kymri's superior had already briefed them without her presence and they were being dismissed. On seeing her arrival, their gazes turned to her, mirroring the judgments of the council members.

Madam Councillor approached her, "You'll remain here, Kymri; you're being relieved of duty and your next in command will take over."

"Madam Councillor, I'm fully capable of fulfilling my duties."

"You may think so. In light of your judgments and behavior over this matter, we are not confident that you are."

"Despite the bonding subject, my decision not to allow a stranded human to be destroyed without assessment was sound. I know concerns for safety are rigid, but we also need to protect the thin diplomatic relationships that we have been trying to build."

"I agree, as an individual, Kymri. In light of the news that you are experiencing a heat, it invariably puts your judgment in question, and it has to be addressed. Once the council completes their own investigation, they may decide as you did. Until then we have to relieve you of duty."

Kymri turned toward the harbor. Several of her guard boarded a small skiff preparing to make sail. Overhead, three dragons launched from the towers.

Madam Councillor's voice was heavy with compassion when she spoke, "I am sorry you are experiencing this heat, Kymri. It will be difficult."

Kymri watched the skiff depart, the knot in her stomach tightening.

J ori sighted a small boat on the horizon as he jogged along the hot beach sand. He was headed out to the small spring he'd found, with his water bottle in hand, and exercising to keep his muscles strong despite the inertia of being stranded on an island. Next time someone asked him the ridiculous question of what to bring if you were stranded on a desert island? A water bottle, and a solid supply of protein and sunscreen.

His feet slowed as he watched the boat, trying to discern how big it was. Was it Kymri? Or a possibly rescue ship? Maybe someone noticed his uploads had stopped and the Coast Guard was alerted to search for him. It was difficult to control the rising excitement. If it was a rescue vessel, could they see the island? He forced himself to wait before running back to retrieve the flares from the boat. In case it was Kymri come to visit. He had no idea what her boat looked like; he'd never seen it.

The excitement of rescue warred with his desire to spend more time with her.

He watched, willing it to come faster. A sail became visible and he relaxed as the shape of the vessel became more defined. Not a rescue ship, just a sailboat. It likely would still take some time, so he continued on his errand to procure the fresh drinking water and returned to his camp.

A small boat sailed into his little bay and he wondered why Kymri never had before. She always approached his camp from the opposite side of the island. It was a small boat meant for short trips between islands. Several women disembarked and strode through the water toward his camp. He tensed; the relief that had settled into him earlier fled. They didn't look friendly.

These women weren't dressed as Kymri had been during her visits. These women were dressed for conflict, their weapons clearly visible and much larger. They wore the same cotton clothing Kymri had, but it was over-laid with leather to cover vital areas of their bodies. They looked more like amazon warriors than the usual island dwellers he met before.

Kymri said she was a guardian. She must have removed her own armor before coming into contact with him. Seems once she found the batteries and disposed of them, she must have decided he was no longer a threat.

If these women were still armed to deal with him, clearly not everyone thought he was completely harmless.

Unless Kymri was dangerous enough to not need the armor.

Now his curiosity was on overdrive.

"You are Jori?"

He nodded. "Where is Kymri?"

"We're here to take you from this island."

"Where to?"

The woman that spoke to him looked down her nose that he dared ask her a question. He felt like he was dealing with border patrol.

"Pack your belongings."

"What of my plane?"

"What of it?" the woman shrugged.

"Okay then," he grumbled. "I'll just get my things, won't be a moment."

The other two women were snuffing out his campfire and moving to load the equipment cases into their boat. Jori swiftly dismantled the tent and stowed it and his bedroll then helped move the rest of his cases and boarded the boat without much else said.

There was nothing offered or asked, and he had the distinct impression he didn't have much choice, especially if he wanted off this particular island.

Maybe where they were going had running water and fresh food that wasn't fish and coconuts.

He watched the beach diminish as they sailed out of the small bay, the pilot of their small boat steering the sail and adjusting the rudder with instinctive efficiency. They slid past his grounded little plane, and he was sorry to abandon it. It wasn't fancy, but it had been his mom's, and he'd flown plenty of places in it, especially in his early days of adventure travel with her.

Once the beach and his Cessna were out of sight, he studied his rescuers and debated whether this was actually a rescue trip.

There were all stern and wore similar scowls to Kymri's. Thoughts of island cannibals returned from his earliest days of being stranded.

He wondered where Kymri was. Why wasn't she with them to see him off his island?

They sailed a long time under the blazing sun before another land mass came into view, and he was glad he had the water to drink.

He wished he had a working camera to document all of this. At least he still had his notes, they would have to do. He should have kept up with his sketch work ... Maybe he could try that. That would be something. His thoughts drifted toward the marketability of hand drawn art. Whatever he drew, it wouldn't be the same as video footage or photographs, especially if he found something mythical.

After so many days on the beach, he no longer trusted the memory of the storm and crash. Especially since he'd hit his head and blacked out. The idea of some large beast actually saving his plane was incredibly outlandish. He'd been lucky.

Returning his attention to his rescuers, he considered their appearance. Just the way these ladies were dressed was out of the ordinary. They'd make for some pretty dramatic images aboard this skiff headed for who-knows-where. Drawings wouldn't do it justice, but it was better than nothing.

Chapter 9

H e must have dozed for a time because when he opened his eyes the scenery had drastically changed. Before him was a bustling harbor crowded with boats of all sizes and even several tall ships. It looked like a medieval village spreading out from the coast, up a gentle incline toward massive stone walls rimming impressive structures. Solid blocks butted with sky-high spires that had platforms jutting out of them. He frowned, wondering if they were for small craft or helicopters, but then, if they were, what kind of navigation tech did they use around here? He glanced around the harbor again. They were all sailing craft as far as he could tell. There were no obvious outboard motors.

His chest was tight despite the excitement in his belly.

Were these people an undocumented culture? He found it hard to believe they were, and yet, the 'legend' of the Bermuda triangle wasn't just a legend for him anymore. There really was something that affected digital and magnetic equipment. And given Kymri's attitude about protecting her people...

Maybe he'd hit the treasure chest of discoveries.

Outwardly, he maintained his impassive stance, looking straight ahead to where they were pulling up to dock. On the inside, he was roiling havoc. It was real, or he was delirious after too long on the island.

His eyes scanned the docks for Kymri. She was nowhere in sight. Her lack of presence tempered his excitement with concern.

Jori's escort led him through the harbor front, by-passing a central market. Markets were one of those places that stood the test of culture and time. Stalls, colors, sounds, smells. The market thrived with trade - they obviously weren't a completely closed society; some stalls had books, magazines and newspapers, while others had jeans, sneakers and various other types of clothing, and one entire stall was dedicated to cosmetics— bright shades of nail polish pulled his attention. The colors reminded him of Kymri. The small sampling of the population which he could see were all dressed in loose cotton clothes in every color one could think of.

There was no time to see much else, as he was led directly to a path that climbed up toward the citadel. As soon as he passed through the thick gate posts most of the city sounds fell away, and the roar of the ocean became muffled beyond the stone barrier.

Walking some distance along a cloister around an open courtyard with fruit trees and walking paths, he was taken through another gated wall to a low building resembling a barracks - or a prison. His heart dropped.

"These will be your accommodations until the council decides otherwise."

The door closed behind him. The lock sounded unnaturally loud in the confined space.

He stared at the room. As far as prisons went, it wasn't so bad. The room was fairly wide, with a bed, table and chairs. Plenty of fresh air and light filtering in through the stone lattice lining the upper portion of the wall. Despite the fact there were no windows facing outward, he could hear the sea beyond. He dropped his backpack on the bed. Through a side door, there was a semi-open space, walled in the same stone lattice. Light and air passed through, but visibility was hindered. A low, sloped roof sheltered the space from the intense tropical sun.

He hoped they would bring him something other than fish and coconuts to eat, if they fed him at all. For all he knew they'd taken him here to forget about.

He drew in a deep breath, deflecting thoughts of imprisonment.

He'd get through this. He always did.

A third door opened into a small, rough bathroom. He kicked off his shoes, worked the levers to get the water flowing, then stripped down and reveled in the first shower he'd had in forever.

"Tell me which barracks he's in."

"Not until they've finished searching his vessel and the reports are in."

"You won't find weapons, I already searched it."

"We will see."

Kymri scowled, pacing the office of her superior, Guardian Liaison Launia.

"Sit. Don't push your luck, Kymri, my patience only extends so far."

She cast her a glance, quickly reading the seriousness of her statement, and settled into the nearest chair so they could still talk.

"Your mother has been to see me."

Kymri didn't respond.

"She's working to have you reinstated as soon as all of this passes."

Her brow went up. "I know you're close friends, but she meddles too much."

The older woman shrugged, "She means well, and only wants what is best for you Kymri."

"Does she? I wonder sometimes that she can see beyond her own ambitions."

"Careful, now."

She swallowed her next retort, turning her attention back to the wide-open windows.

"If there's nothing found, you have nothing to worry about—you know this," Launia said.

She did. She didn't know why she was so tense. Something wasn't right; she could feel it like a nettle that was wedged in such a way it couldn't be seen, just felt enough for it to be bothersome.

Resisting the urge to resume pacing, her fingers drummed her knee trying to rein in her agitation. "With the mating bond started, they can't destroy him."

The older woman looked up from her sheaf of papers, her brow furrowed, "if they deem him a threat to our people, he will be destroyed." She shrugged, "probably not until you've conceived, and the heat has passed."

Kymri's heart flailed in her chest. She didn't want to conceive. She wanted Jori alive.

She was on her feet pacing again, trying to figure out a way to keep him safe as well as protect her people.

Dammit, she shouldn't have to protect one from the other. But she did have to. "What do you see as my options?" she asked the older woman.

She replaced the reports on her desk giving Kymri her full attention again, steepling her fingers as she thought. "His motivation for coming here was to expose us, he can't be trusted not to once he leaves."

Kymri considered trying to convince him to keep their secret. Would he? Could she show him how important their safety was and that protecting their existence depended on invisibility? Could she plead with him? She'd never pleaded with anyone in her life and it left an acrid sensation in the back of her throat. If it meant having Jori, and protecting her queen and her people too, she would do it.

There was a knock on the door before Zayli entered.

"Madame, Guardian Marli hasn't returned from her patrol, and we're unable to locate her."

"When did she fly out?"

"Two patrol rotations ago." She turned an accusatory glare on Kymri. "We weren't sure if she was following Kymri's example and lingering during her route. She hasn't returned as yet, and follow up patrols haven't been able to find a sign of her. She's disappeared."

"She wouldn't do that." Kymri shot to her feet, heart pounding, "Madame, let me help find her. We can send out two patrols of three guardians arching in opposite directions to cover more air at a faster rate."

Her superior considered her a moment then gave a sharp nod.

She and Zayli jogged back to the guard tower to prepare for flight.

"You should stay behind, you're too distracted," Zayli snarled at Kymri.

"My loyalty was never in question."

"Wasn't it? Really, Kymri? Looks to me like you put a human male before the concerns of your people."

"It wasn't like that."

"As far as the rest of us are concerned, it was. We can't trust you'll have our back."

"Don't be ridiculous."

Zayli stopped, forcing Kymri to do likewise, "Yeah? And what will you do when we find out Marli's disappearance has something to do with *him*?"

"Why would it?"

"He had back up batteries for his equipment stowed aboard his plane, Kymri. He still had the capability to expose us and still does, so long as he is breathing. Your selfish stupidity puts all of us, and our queen, at risk."

Kymri's heart dropped. She drew a breath and resumed jogging toward the guard tower, Zayli close behind.

As soon as they reached the tower, Kymri gave the orders to prepare for spiral-net search pattern and several of the crew immediately came forward to prepare.

They stripped off their cotton garb in the change room and stepped onto the platform in threes with enough space between them to shift. Kymri stood in center position and had begun shifting into her dragon form when a dull, deep pain knotted her lower stomach, dropping her to her knees.

The women flanking her turned in concern, but she held out a hand to stay them, her body quivering, the magic swirling around her. It felt different, like she'd suddenly been altered. The knot in her belly tightened, then relaxed a fraction. Something remained. It felt like someone lodged their fist through her belly.

Able to catch her breath despite the discomfort, she completed the shift, letting her magic run its course through her body until her dragon joined the two to either side of her. They launched and veered into their search flight pattern, moving counter clockwise to their usual patrol pattern. The crew following would take the usual route, fanned out to cover more air as they went. They would cross paths with each revolution.

Kymri prayed they found Marli.

A second knot, one of worry, settled on top of the first hardened knot in her belly. Struggling to keep up with her crew, she strained to fly faster to remain abreast and floundered halfway through the return revolution. Gritting her teeth, she completed the route.

They found nothing. And when they angled for approach to the platform, her wings wavered and she barely made the landing, her legs and knees hitting the stone hard, sending her tumbling over herself and slamming into the interior wall, losing consciousness.

Kymri's head swam and pounded when tried to open her eyes or turn her head. Dragging an arm up off the bed to within view, she could see she was bandaged. She ached all over and her belly contained a dull weight.

"Wha-what happened?" her voice was weak.

A face loomed over her, peering into her eyes, "try not to move, you'll be fine. Had a close call but all is well." The face scrunched into a smile, "you just need to rest for a little while."

Lifting her head, her vision wavered as she struggled to focus on her surroundings. The infirmary. The shaman that spoke to her wandered out of the room and a new figure took up space in front of her. Easing her head back, she waited for her mother's face to come into focus.

Kolina stood, hands clasped behind her straight back, dressed in her usual Queen's Guard formal-functional garb. Once her head and vision stilled, Kymri saw her mother's usually staunchly thinned lips were quirked at the corner and her calculating eyes were sparkling.

She couldn't recall the last time she'd seen Kolina look 'happy'.

"Oh, dear dragon goddess, what have you done now?" Kymri groaned.

"It's not what *I've* done, little one. It's what *you've* done."

Kymri's mind went blank. Then the buzzing in her ears started. What had Kolina wanted of her?

No.

Shit.

Oh no.

"What's wrong with me? Why can't I get up?"

"Your body is recovering from the shock of shifting while impregnated. The shamans are very impressed with you. Most dragonesses can't shift at all, let alone shift and then do a two-hour patrol. It seems the little youngling created a shell to protect itself from being crushed during your transformation."

Kymri stared at her mother's glee.

"Anyway," she continued, "you over-exerted yourself and very nearly missed the landing platform. You made it, although a little banged up. You just need to rest, and you'll be up and around."

"I hate being confined," she growled.

"I know." Kolina patted her arm.

Kymri stared at her mother's hand on her arm. She rarely touched her. Her eyes flicked back to Kolina's face. She was practically glowing.

"This is a bad dream, or I'm hallucinating."

"Not at all, the shamans said there was no need to drug you. And I strongly advise against trying to get up too soon," she said when Kymri tried to push herself up onto her elbows but ended up dropping back onto her pillow with a groan.

"I have to—Marli hasn't been found yet," she panted from the small exertion.

"The others are out, widening the search net." a frown finally settled over Kolina's features. "You just stay comfortable." The patting returned.

"This isn't comfortable, *Mother*, it feels like I have a stone in my uterus."

"Really!" Kolina breathed, "Oh this is better than expected. She will be strong!"

Who was this woman? Or had one of her rivals finally succeeded in slipping something into her food?

"Shaman? I think I'm hallucinating." Kymri called out, while trying to lean away from her mother's patting hand. She didn't think she could handle anymore, and began trying to think of anything that would send her away.

She just woke to find herself impregnated, and her mother had lost her mind.

An image of Jori came into her mind, halting all other thoughts along with her breath.

Fear crept over her and she gasped at the intensity of it.

He fathered her child.

The bonding hadn't knotted yet.

Would he want to know?

What if the child were male?

Her hand slid over her womb.

She hadn't wanted this. She really hadn't.

But here it was.

The only two choices were to raise the child or give it away.

She knew humans had methods to create another choice. Kymri's dragon wouldn't allow for that, nor would her society. And neither did she, she knew deep down.

It also wasn't part of her culture to consider the sire much beyond conception either.

Her dragon wanted her to bring Jori into the fold, and so did she.

Chapter 10

J ori paced the little stone-screened yard, walking trenches in the once-grass covered dirt.

There was trouble.

He'd heard his guards talking about a disappearance and when they came to check on him, their hostility had increased ten-fold. "You're lucky Kymri Steelscale is fighting to keep you alive," one snarled at him while handing him food.

She was fighting for him?

What had he done to incur a death sentence?

Thinking back on their island encounters, he remembered when she threatened him with a knife. The batteries. She destroyed the batteries to protect her people. He and his equipment were a threat to this insular culture. Apparently enough to decide it was worth his life.

He peered through the curled openings of the stone lattice walls surrounding him. It was near impossible to see much of anything. He had been able to make out large, dark shapes gliding in the distance. He could hear the sound of the wind when they passed close by. He couldn't quite make out what they were. Gliders maybe? The shape wasn't quite right. If he were delusional, he'd say they looked more like dragons than anything. But then he chalked that up to much too much time alone, first on the island, now confined to this prison and with those combined with his mother's stories—delusion. He ignored the whisper of his sub-conscious, reminding him of the large object he met in the sky that day.

He sighed as he continued looking for weak points in the stonework. Figuring out a way home kept his mind occupied. It wasn't good to dwell too much about how trapped he was, and on the flip side of that, nor did it help to think too much about Kymri. Although she was a more pleasant distraction from thoughts of rotting away in this place, being constantly aroused wasn't helpful either.

He tried to reserve thoughts and fantasies of Kymri for when he went to bed, and he could fall asleep to her mental image. He was growing a little concerned about the obsessive turn his mind was taking. This wasn't like him; he didn't obsess over women. But it seemed she was all he could think about and focus on. As much as he wanted out of this place, he wanted to be with her or take her away from here with him. Any scenario played out with the two of the together - anywhere.

The familiar sound of rushing wind came around from the coastal side of his prison. Darting to the wall, he pressed in close to align his sight with the where he thought the thing was that created the rushing noise. There were several flying in formation, as they glided in closer and banked, he was finally able to catch a glimpse. They held the same shape as the mystery birds he'd seen flying overhead while he was on the island. They hadn't come in this close before and they were flying in the opposite direction from those he'd seen in the distance before.

His breath lodged in his throat. Either he'd finally gone crazy, or those were fucking dragons. Excitement bounced in his gut. They were real! They were fucking real!

They glided out of sight and his hands shot up to his head, clutching at his hair.

His Cessna had met its destruction from a collision with a fucking dragon!

He'd been right - his mother's stories were true. He needed to document this somehow. On impulse he went to his backpack for his camera, excitement overriding his logic for a moment.

"Fuck."

Reality came crashing in just as fast. No camera, phone or recording device.

He dropped to sit on the edge of the bed.

Dragons were real.

This is what Kymri was willing to pull a knife on him for. And here he was, his first impulse was to document it to share with the world. This is exactly why he was locked in this place. Because they knew he would expose them.

What would it cost them?

He wasn't just chasing a fantasy anymore. Now he was faced with the fact these creatures were real, and they were here because they were protected, and these people were willing to protect them with their lives.

Why would they do that?

They must have some kind of relationship with them and in order to have that, they must be sentient.

Had a dragon saved him too —the night of the storm?

Jori scrubbed a hand over his face, reeling, his hands shook.

Reaching into his pack, he extracted his notebook, flipping through it absently as a distraction while his mind adjusted. His eyes slid over drawings of his wrecked plane, landscapes on the island, birds - he'd drawn the outline of the mystery birds high overhead. He could see much more clearly now that they were the same shape as the large beasts he'd just witnessed gliding past his wall. He flipped a few more pages and there was his drawing of the constellation. The stars in the shape of an elegant curving dragon, similar in shape to the silhouette of those he'd just seen. With the book in his upturned hands, his tattoos were visible on his inner forearms. The tattoos taken from his mother's artwork.

He hadn't seen it before. He couldn't explain why he hadn't seen it before. There it was. Those same shapes were represented in the tattoos. The same outline, the pinpoints of the stars, obscured by the colors of cosmic space dust and tropical flowers.

Had his mother seen these images in books? Or had she actually been here before?

His heart began thumping harder. Something in him whispered that she had.

But when? His mind raced, trying to remember all the places she'd described to him when he was young.

She said she planned to explore this region, not that she already had. She'd always referred to them as mythological or legendary places. And while she had talked about the legends related to this area, she hadn't told him that she had in reality been here before.

She must have been here before his birth, or while he was too young to remember? It was like she was leading him to these fantastical places without making it real. Why? If she'd been here before, why wouldn't she just bring him back with her? Why mask it?

He let a thumb slide over the colorful image anchored into his flesh. Most of his tattoos were facsimiles of her semi-abstract art.

Pulling off his shirt, he inspected each one within his view. Without a reflective surface, he couldn't see the ones adorning his back and shoulders. One of the ones on his abdomen he could recognize as an obscure representation of the shape of the island and its citadel. The first view he saw on approaching the harbor.

Christ.

What else was hidden in her art?

He was excited to suddenly see into the thought of her art though felt pretty damned stupid for not having seen it before now. She was a deliberate and thoughtful woman, of course there was meaning hidden in the images.

He knew this of her. Now, he realized, there was so much more of her he didn't know. And likely wouldn't ever. Especially from his father - he never spoke of her, not since she disappeared. Unless Jori pushed on a subject, but even then it wouldn't be long before he shut the conversation down and walked away. And that's basically what their relationship was like - since she disappeared.

Before she disappeared, the three of them were very close. He was a happy kid. After... It was like he lost both parents at once.

Jori stared at the images he'd drawn in his notebook and tried to correlate them with the images on his skin.

He was trying to shift his way of viewing his past from the eyes of a child and adolescent to how he thought now as an adult.

What did he really know of his mother?

Kymri hated being confined, but the shamans had insisted she stay abed for at least a couple more days to allow her body and her magic to recover. The only reason she obeyed was because of the newly realized life growing inside her. Propped up in her bed she painted her nails with the vibrant metallic hot pink nail polish and glanced through several fashion magazines smuggled from the continent.

Marli was still missing and the council were growing more and more tense. They refused to let her participate in the search patrols. Reluctantly, she had to admit to herself, after that last round, she probably wouldn't be able to do a proper job of it.

Kolina's presence was sparse. Security around the queen tightened even more than it was before.

Now the guards were trying to determine if Jori had any connection to the dragons. The male dragons had been quiet for so long, she had to admit, she'd grown a little relaxed in the last decade, but she would never say that they'd grown careless.

At least she hadn't until now, when her compassion and her 'heat' kicked in.

The island was facing an 'intruder' and a missing dragoness. She was pregnant and relieved of duty.

This was not a good time. Everything was falling apart all at once, and she didn't know what to try to fix first.

Obviously, the pregnancy couldn't be fixed. Not until the child was ready to emerge.

As much as she had bonded with Jori, a bond which was still not yet complete, she didn't know if she could fully trust him. How could she know he was genuine, and not just infiltrating? If that were the case, then he'd done a mighty fine job of fooling her and twisting her around his finger. She'd gone full in for him and was teetering on completely loyal mate devotion and utter humiliation.

She was a guardian commander for dragonsakes! This was so far below her; it was no wonder she'd been removed from command. She deserved it.

Her people really were at risk, and she hadn't been able to see it, she was so lost in lust and hormonal shift.

And her mother! Her mother was gleeful for its consequences.

Kymri never in her life would have thought that her mother wanted grandchildren. Never. She'd barely been a mother to her, how could she have guessed? Was she desperate to make up for lost motherly bonding, she was hoping to do it with Kymri's offspring?

She dropped back on to her pillow, blowing out her breath, staring up at the ornately carved beams supporting the arched ceiling.

She still felt like her uterus harbored a stone.

She was in such a mess.

She couldn't even go to her best friend Marli because she was still missing, and it may be her fault.

She'd let down her guard.

If she'd been facing one of her subordinates, she not only would have had them relieved of duty, she might have even banished her.

Perhaps that's what she should do. Leave. No longer fit to serve her queen and people.

If she bore a dragoness, she could give her to her mother. But her dragon didn't like that idea.

If she bore a male child... then what?

Her breath lodged in her chest. Then what? Her mind seemed to go blank. She didn't know.

Her dragon didn't like the idea of sending away a male child either. And she knew he wouldn't be welcome on the island. He wouldn't be forbidden, nor would he be welcome.

Male younglings were sent away to live with their fathers, given to a tribe that takes male children or abandoned ones.

Her dragon growled.

Normally Kymri's dragon was silent on things, lately, with the excess hormones driving her natural instincts, she was become more proactive in Kymri's choices.

How long had it been since she actually took her dragon's wishes into account? Maybe she should be asking why her dragon had sunk to the back of her consciousness for so long?

Maybe because she'd become such a damned control freak, she'd been shutting her dragon out. And now in matters of dragon importance, her dragon was making her wishes known.

Maybe it was time to listen. Maybe this is why she was so out of balance with the coming of her heat.

Her mother, and the archival books, had said that metal dragons sometimes did this when out of balance, allowing her ambition to silence what never should be. She wasn't in true union with her dragon. She used her warrior nature but repressed everything else to her will. Apparently, her dragon had had enough of that, when faced with the opportunity to complete her dragon duty by having offspring. No matter how hard she'd tried to deny it and take control of her own life, her body and her instinct had decided otherwise.

What of Jori?

Could she trust her choice?

She'd been raised to mistrust males. They were the enemy, and were only good for procreation. Kymri never wanted to destroy him. She never wanted to mate for life and procreate either. But now she'd bonded, which meant in effect, life. And procreated, which also meant life.

Female or male child.

The sex does not matter, no matter what the current tradition is. We could leave if our youngling was not acceptable.

Kymri's insides turn upside down. She couldn't even think about leaving. She couldn't abandon her queen and her people.

Our queen would understand.

Would she?

My duty is to protect her, with my life. Nothing else matters except the continuation of my queen's life and safety, she told her dragon.

She could practically feel her dragon roll her eyes at her. *I know that. The Council are the ones who decided that male children should leave. The queen had male children and had to sacrifice her relationship with them to protect her people. She can't leave. You can if they pressure you.*

You are not royalty; we are not tied to this island.

I don't want to leave. It's my home.

What is more important? Your home, or your child?

Kymri looked down at her flat stomach. She could still feel the hard weight inside her womb.

She couldn't decide that so quickly.

Until she'd only just discovered the pregnancy, she had not wanted children at all. And now she was being faced with a decision to keep the child, or not, to leave her home, or not. How could she decide so quickly?

Was it like this for all dragonesses?

She wondered.

Her mother had told her she hadn't wanted a child either.

Kymri had figured that out long ago.

She saw how other dragonesses had been so close and bonded to their young. Marli's mother was very close to her; they were nearly inseparable.

Her throat suddenly thickened. Each time she'd witnessed Marli and her mother's relationship, she'd always found an excuse to leave them alone and find other things to do.

Kymri strove to ignore how this made her feel.

She'd had her mother there. She was present in her way. There was just no emotional bond between them. Their relationship was a thin thread of genetics and proximity.

Resentment clawed up her chest. It was familiar, she'd felt it many times, but it didn't serve her, so she swallowed it back down. She didn't want to be bitter and resentful.

She just wanted to fulfill her duty to her people and her queen. This was her identity.

Emotions complicated things.

She was just the best guardian she could be.

Simple. Uncomplicated. Straightforward, that was all.

This was her life mission.

Everything else was a distraction.

And yet she was now facing the fact that she could no longer keep life as simple and straightforward as she wanted to.

Biology and instinct muddied her path.

And she wasn't happy about it.

Her dragon growled.

Kymri understood that her control was tenuous. If the dragon decided to overrule her, she could, and she would. It was best to live in harmony, compromise. And she supposed the dragon had decided Kymri had been in the cockpit for long enough.

Just give me some time.

Dragon huffed.

Please.

Dragon groaned, and Kymri accepted that as a concession.

What do I do now?

In such a short time, her life had been turned upside down and she didn't know what she wanted really. Well kind of. But she didn't know what to do about it, how to reconcile what she really wanted now, that she hadn't known she wanted, with what her society would allow.

She closed her eyes and drew a deep breath, to cleanse her muddled mind and focus.

What do I want? What did I want? No, what do I want now?

I want Jori.

She took a deep breath, letting it out slowly and shakily.

She'd never 'wanted' a man before.

She did now.

Next?

I want to stay with my people.

That hadn't changed.

She breathed a little easier.

And.

I want to keep a child and grow a relationship with him or her.

Wow.

Never in a million generations would she have thought she'd ever, ever admit that.

Her dragon purred.

How can I have all of these things at once? They don't work together. I have to choose.

We shall see.

What do you know that I don't?

Now that you are listening to me, you'll learn so much more about yourself that you didn't allow room for in the past.

I see.

Kymri, we are more than duty and talons and guardians and protectors.

We can also be mothers and mates.

It's too complicated. They won't accept what I want.

Make them.

How?

Prove to them it can work. It did at one time.

Until it didn't anymore—that's how we're in this situation in the first place.

Yes, but it doesn't have to stay this way forever.

Kymri snorted. Have you met the Council?

I was semi-dormant, not dead. I am well aware of the past and current situation on this island. Listen to me. It's time for change. Other dragons will support this.

Are you telling me to revolt against the Council and the queen?

No. I'm telling you to talk to them and find reasons to see this alternative path.

You're telling me to become a politician and a diplomat.

If necessary.

Kymri groaned. This is what her mother wanted.

She isn't wrong.

I don't want this. You just told me to figure out what I wanted, and now you're telling me to do something I really don't want to do.

She could feel her dragon shrug.

Kymri growled.

Her dragon chuckled. *Welcome to the next phase of your life, little one.*

It sucks.

Agreed.

Chapter 11

S tenlen and his wingmen were out again.

"We'll find the damned island if it kills us," he growled.

"Not looking forward to the repercussions if we don't," Merwin said.

"The king expects results. And if we want to maintain our status, we have to produce results."

His job was to find the females. That was fine by him. He liked the chase.

He didn't like having his time wasted, so long as his efforts produced results, then it was all good.

"I can't believe we lost that little bitch, Sten, it doesn't make any sense, we had her," Clive complained.

Following her original trajectory, they soared in a large arc trying to pick up a scent.

"Smell that? I think we've got a ripe one!" Clive's voice oozed glee.

Not the same dragoness as before, a deliciously different scent, having passed through here not long before their arrival, just long enough she was out of sight.

Altering course, they trailed it, like they did last time, only shifting altitude, climbing so that they'd be above her when they sighted her.

She wouldn't spot them before they got her locked in.

Their persistence was paying off.

The thrill of giddiness when another scent crossed the first.

Stenlen signaled to climb again.

Soon small shapes were visible in the distance. A snarl erupted from his throat, echoed by his wingmen.

"I can taste them," Clive said with a growl.

Holding back the pursuit, there were more - three of them. "We're close to their central territory." He drifted to the side of their arch, watching their direction.

He scented the land before he saw the ribbon cutting the blue sky from the glittering surface of the water.

Below them, from the other direction, three more figures appeared. They were crisscrossing in spiraling arcs to cover their territory.

They had to move fast. Even though they were well above them, the air currents would drag the scent of the male dragons, giving away their presence. He angled again and drove toward the projected center of their arcs. Toward the land.

In moments, a citadel came into view, buildings rolling outward down toward the coastline of the main island. Now to get a better look at this place and its fortifications.

A deep baritone sound rippled across the island.

Jori recognized it as some kind of alarm.

Within moments there were shapes racing through the air beyond his lattice stone wall. He couldn't see clearly what was happening, the sounds of growling and roaring were so loud the stone beneath his hands vibrated.

He watched through the openings in the wall for any activity. A pair of dragons engaged in combat grappled and tumbled through the air until a third joined in to attack the larger intruder. The newcomer clamped powerful jaws on the larger dragon's throat while the other continued to keep its dangerous claws occupied as they struggled to stay airborne.

They fell out of his range of sight, but after long noisy moments the ground shook with an incredible crash, the larger dragon must have broken free, for it flew off, circling past the cliff-top prison Jori was housed in.

The two smaller dragons didn't give chase, then several more came soaring out of the sky, chasing the larger one out of range.

After several more moments, the air went quiet except for the occasional rush of air from one of them circling overhead.

Jori dropped onto his cot.

Holy shit.

His hands shook and his heart pounded, the rushing of his blood loud in his ears.

Fear and exhilaration pumped adrenaline through his body. There was something about the sounds of their growls and roars that pulled at his skin.

The islanders had been attacked by a much larger dragon than their defenders. Fear for Kymri's safety rushed through him. This island was under threat, of much larger dragons. What kind of damage could it have done without the protection of this fleet of smaller dragons?

How could these people live with that kind of threat looming over them?

K ymri heard the alarm. Her bare feet hit the cool stone floor and she was running for the guard tower. As she emerged from the room, she merged with the rush of other bodies running through the corridors to perform emergency duties during times of crisis. Everyone had a place to be and a roll to fulfill.

With a glance, she saw the shamans moving the younglings down into the lower levels of the citadel closer to the evacuation caves. She knew that the villagers would be gathering their families and making their way toward the citadel. The merchants would be locking down their valuables under the flagstone floors of their simple houses. Many of the inhabitants on the island were human - neighbors and friends that needed the protection of the dragons. Theirs was a peaceful co-existence. Some of the dragonesses lived in the village among them rather than among the citadel's warrior and ruling classes.

Her body was running for the guard tower, her mind went out toward Jori. He was confined to the prison barracks at the far end of the complex.

Duty kept her moving toward the launch tower. It was her job to protect the island and the queen. Once she reached the upper levels of the guard tower, she could see the chaotic order of the guardians. Everyone was on alert, shifting and launching into action.

"How many?" she barked.

"Three."

Kymri stripped her clothing and shifted.

Pain tore through her body radiating outward from her womb. The hard shell around the child crackled and thickened, taking up more space inside her. It was protecting itself from her magic. She gasped for breath while the sharpness of the pain subsided enough for her to focus on what she was trying to do.

As soon as she could draw a deep enough breath, she went for the ledge and threw out her wings. Gaining altitude, she could see where two of the intruders were being engaged by her sister guardians. She circled the island looking for the third. Circling upward, high above the citadel, movement on the opposite side of the skirmishes drew her attention. Zayli was fighting alone with another of the larger intruders. No matter their differences, a sister guardian was still a sister. They always protected their own —no matter what. And she wouldn't be able to hold up for long on her own.

Kymri tucked in her wings and dove with a snarl.

She ignored the throbbing in her lower belly drilling all her focus into a weak point of the intruder's throat and clamped onto it with the full weight and force of her diving body. Her jaws closed on his scales and squeezed hard.

He roared and reared against her attack; his claws still tangled up with Zayli. Kymri clamped a talon on one of his wings and they began to tumble.

The ground rushed toward them, jagged rocks and frothing sea below the cliff-top prison barracks. Kymri wrenched hard, pulling their falling masses away from the stone building, but the writhing of the intruder, wrenched them back again, causing them to collide with the jagged cliff wall. The impact loosened her hold on his throat, and Zayli took the brunt of the impact, her head slamming back into the solid rock wall. She fell as the intruder shook himself free.

Kymri's strength began to flag and she was losing altitude. There wasn't enough strength in her to chase him, instead she dropped down to Zayli's inert form.

Zayli lay on her back on the hard rocks. Kymri hoped her scales were strong enough to prevent penetration, but the impact could do serious internal damage. Her body shook with the exertion of the fight and holding her shift. She held her dragon form despite her waning strength and slipped her body between Zayli's and the rocks and surging ocean to keep her head out of the water.

Someone would find them; she knew her sisters would search the islands. And sure enough, two more swooped into view overhead to pursue the fleeing intruder. A third surveying the area spotted them and left. Kymri knew she was going to get help. She sighed under the strain of holding her form. She just had to hold it until they returned.

Dragonsdammit, this child was going to be the death of her.

She was starting to lose consciousness when she heard the whoosh of air over head. Sliding out from under Zayli's dragon form, she clung to one of the boulders as she slid back into her human form, giving in to darkness again.

Great, she was going to be forced to spend even more time in fucking bed, she thought as she blacked out.

Chapter 12

———

The door to Jori's prison wrenched open, and two angrier than usual guards crowded the space.

While lying on the bed, he'd been sketching in his notebook. On seeing their expressions, he put it down and stood. Their faces were pinched, and he could feel the rage rolling toward him. One clenched her fist around her spear, the other had both hands curled into very tight fists at her sides.

"Out."

Eying both warily as he passed, he kept his back straight and squared his shoulders.

It was several days after the attack and escape of the large dragon outside his prison.

Obviously, things were still tense on the island.

All the way through the complex, he remained ready in case one of his prison guards decided lash out at him, but neither did.

They walked him along corridor after corridor through the belly of the citadel, then up several sets of winding staircases and along several wider corridors where the architecture was distinctly different from that of the lower levels. Here the ceiling rested on carved arches capping equally ornate pillars. The walls were covered in massive paintings and tapestries. It was like one of the castles restored to the medieval period which he'd visited in Europe. Torches flickering in sconces lined the path, and the smell of the burning pitch was heavy in the air.

He was led to massive double doors. His guard with the spear thumped her weapon on the stone floor and the doors slowly whispered open on well-oiled hinges.

His shoulders tensed as the room opened to him beyond the doors.

He stepped in. The air crackled. The sensation of power whispered over his flesh and slithered down his spine.

The cavernous room was full of light from the large arched windows. At one end, set against a solid wall, was a raised dais where stood an ornately dragon-carved throne occupied by the upright figure of a woman. She was surrounded by what was clearly her guard. The space between him and the dais was filled with a circular version of the House of Lords. A podium faced him with its back to the dais, and from either side of that, semi-circular rows of seats faced the central raised witness box.

He took a deep breath. This couldn't be good.

His eyes drifted away from the faces turned toward him up toward the banners hung from the ceiling. The familiarity of the symbols nudged him like an old memory.

His guards walked him to the enclosed witness box in the center of the room. As he made his way along the room, he realized he was the only man. The gate was opened for him to step up into it. It was made to face the speaker at eye level. The queen looked on from above her, her expression one of mild curiosity.

He was grossly under dressed in his khakis and Beatles tee-shirt.

He dropped his gaze and bowed before her.

He straightened, hiking boots planted at shoulder width, head high.

Maybe now he'd get a better understanding of what these people were all about. He'd barely been spoken to since he was 'rescued' from the little island that he now thought of as his and Kymri's. Given what little he'd seen of the people here, and Kymri's protective attitude over her people, and that his trip had led him straight to a prison, he hoped they weren't going to decide he could spend the rest of his life there.

From his earlier interactions with Kymri, he understood now that his plan to document the legends of this culture put them at risk. And after having seen the beasts in the skies around his prison, he knew why.

Would they even consider letting him go home? He wasn't optimistic, especially not when he considered the expressions of nearly every person in this room. It wasn't looking good for him at all.

Kymri had pulled a knife on him over some batteries. The guards were armed. These people weren't peace loving hippies. They have something great to protect. He swallowed, his head level as he faced the speaker and the queen, adopting the expression and posture he'd learned from his father when meeting a new semester of students at the university.

Don't show an ounce of fear or they'll eat you alive.

He drew in a deep steady breath, letting confidence and patience descend over him. His mother's curiosity simmered below the surface. He was at the very heart of their culture. Not as an observer, but an experiencer.

He resisted the urge to look for Kymri among the unwelcoming faces. He hadn't seen her among the other women. The desire to see her rose up so hard and fast within him he clenched his fists to control it and focus his attention on the proceedings before him. His life likely depended on it.

"Jori Mountainside, you have been brought before Her Majesty's Council for the purpose of determining your motives in entering our territory uninvited."

Fair enough.

The speaker launched into a summary of what he supposed was Kymri's account of their interactions. Reports of his location were read out to the room at large. He wasn't sure how they would know that as he hadn't seen a single person other than Kymri, until his escort arrived the day he was moved off the small island. Then he recalled the mystery birds, and how they very likely were the beasts he'd seen outside his prison. Were they sentient enough to provide reports with that kind of detail?

The recounting went on, and his cheeks burned when the subject of his deepening relationship with Kymri was orated. His eyes darted to the queen; her curious gaze turned amused. He hadn't expected that to be part of the report. He drew a deep breath to clear his surprise embarrassment, returning his attention to the speaker's monologue.

"We have brought you here to account for these actions and provide your perspective of these events."

He swallowed, considering how much to say. If he lied or held back, would they feed him to one of the beasts? He shuddered at the thought of being impaled on the spiked teeth and crushed by the powerful jaws.

The speaker's brow rose at the long moment of his silence.

He cleared his throat, "the report is correct. That is what happened."

She nodded, accepting his statement. "Why are you here, Jori Mountainside?"

Those were the words Kymri had asked him. Why was he there?

"I flew out over the Atlantic Ocean off the coast of Charleston, South Carolina to determine if the myths of the Bermuda Triangle and the mysterious beasts residing within it were true."

No one spoke, waiting for him to continue.

Why?

He thought over his next words, "The plane I flew belonged to my mother. She bought it when I was a child, and it was the beginning of our adventures together. We traveled around the world, exploring mystical myths and locations, often traveling by that plane. My father wanted me to become an academic like he is. But after my mother disappeared 20 years ago, continuing on these explorative journeys were a way to keep her memory alive. So, it became my calling. I started doing video diaries and making documentaries. I record everything I do and photograph every place and its people so that it can be compiled into a book to be published and shared with the world. The income helps fund more projects like the one I intended to do when I ended up here."

"You came here to exploit us for your personal gain."

He jerked, stung.

"Madam, that's not how I saw it when I took off from Charleston."

"How did you see it?"

"I thought I might, if I was lucky, spot some 'dinosaur age' creature that would scientifically account for the mythical beasts. As for a potential culture—if anything, maybe an abandoned island with weather-worn hints of ancient peoples etched into the crumbling stones." He swallowed, his throat as dry as the week he'd spent in the Sahara after his camel ran away. "I never thought I'd find both alive and thriving."

"What places have you traveled to?"

Jori thought a moment. There'd been so many throughout his life. Once he began his litany, it went on for some time. Mountainous villages in the east where his mother taught him to climb so they could see the tombs of the ancients. He learned how to wield a machete in the Amazon jungle during an expedition to find deep valley pyramids. Sand blown desert villages abandoned millennia ago. There was one visit to the far north, he shuddered and avoided that memory. He hated the cold almost as much as thieving polar bears. Other locations, other remote islands. All places that held ancient mysteries attached to them.

"And the beasts? You found them at each place?"

Jori smiled then, "No Ma'am. Not one."

"Then why would you continue to travel to so many places, failing your purpose?"

Again, he thought about his response.

"My mother started us on these journeys, I never had the chance to understand why. But when we traveled, although we went to many places, she always took me into the vicinity of where the creatures were said to have lived. Maybe it was for safety? I couldn't say for sure. We usually visited the villages in the general area, meeting the people and learning their cultures. There were incredible experiences to have grown up with and I count myself fortunate to have been exposed to so many different places and types of people."

"What manner of creatures was she seeking?"

"They all seemed to be variations of dragons."

"Your mother had a deeply ingrained obsession with dragons?"

Jori shrugged, "They were her passion, yes. She made a lot of art centered on them." He held up his forearm, "I had some of her pieces turned into tattoos—this one here," he pointed and traced the image, "seems to match the constellation in this territory, which isn't visible anywhere else on earth that I'm aware of."

There were a few murmurs among those gathered on the stands.

"And now that I'm in this room, the symbols on these banners look familiar. It's possible they too are in her artwork."

"If this is true, that would mean that your mother has knowledge of this place."

"I would have to agree, Ma'am. But I wasn't aware of this until after I arrived here and began to notice the similarities."

Movement on the dais caught Jori's eye. The queen raised a hand and one of her guard leaned in to hear her speak. The guard stepped forward "Madam Speaker, the queen wishes to know how old Jori Mountainside is."

"Please answer Her Majesty," the speaker said to Jori.

"Thirty-Two."

The queen spoke to her guard again. "Madam Speaker, Her Majesty would like Jori Mountainside to approach the dais."

The speaker inclined her head, and Jori's escorts stepped forward. One opened the booth and moved aside so he could step down, then they both fell in place beside him as they walked around the speaker and approached the dais.

There was shift in the feel of the room as he moved toward the woman on the throne.

The hair on his arms rose and the air around him was alive like he was approaching high voltage generators. His lizard brain whispered 'predator,' which set him on edge. He forced his hands to relax at his sides, preventing them from curling into fists. As an afterthought, his gaze drifted along the wall of well-armed guards.

They stopped, and he looked up into the queen's face.

She was beautiful, in a way that had little to do with the charge of power that surrounded her. Most arresting were her eyes; he was close enough now that he could see that the unusual color held an inner luminescence that denoted her as not *quite* human. She blinked and the glow faded, making her appear human again. With that distraction gone, he studied her features, which held some familiarity to them.

Had he met her before? The possibility was highly unlikely. That familiar nudge pushed at him, as it had the symbols on the overhanging banners. Had his mother painted or sketched this woman?

The queen's eyes were glued to his face.

She stood.

The sounds of a room full of people behind him pulled at his attention. He didn't dare turn around. He didn't know if he was expected to kneel or bow or lower his gaze before her, so instead he stood as he was, feet planted at shoulder width, hands loose at his sides, waiting.

She stepped forward and down several steps, stopping so that she remained above him.

She stared into his eyes, unblinking. He stared back, his breath even and controlled.

Her nostrils flared as he'd seen Kymri's do.

She blinked, breaking the pressure that had begun to bear down on him.

"I wish to see your images".

Images? The tattoos? His gaze dropped to his forearm, the cosmic colors dappling his skin around pinpricks of white representing stars. He lifted his arm and angled it so that she may see it.

Her expression remained impassive, her gaze studied it for several moments.

"There are more?"

He nodded, his hands moving to the hem of his tee-shirt. He hesitated, "may I?"

She nodded.

He turned and removed his shirt, the cool air of the room slid around him, along with acute awareness of being so exposed to a room full of onlookers.

Several of the art pieces were wrapped around his torso or in patches over his back and shoulders. They were mostly abstract pieces with shapes and flowers and vines superimposed in bursts of color.

He turned slowly so that she might look upon him. It was as he finally finished the revolution and faced her again that her gaze slid to the one tattoo that lacked any color at all. Over his heart was the black scripted tattoo of his parents' names, entwined.

"Elora," the queen said on a breath.

Chapter 13

K ymri's heart stalled.

Elora.

A collective gasp hushed through the room.

From the back of the room she had heard the report, and Jori's explanation of his actions.

A pang of protective jealousy had struck her when he approached the queen, and when his shirt had come off, she wanted nothing more than to remove him from the eyes of every woman in the room.

That name changed everything.

Elora.

The queen's immobility where she stood, the power of the name, rippled across the room and Kymri could feel it where she stood. The rawness of it scraped at her heart.

The speaker stood, dismissing the assembly. The doors opened and everyone filed out.

Kymri remained where she was.

Unless the queen commanded her to leave, she would stay close to Jori. Even then, she might disobey. Her breath shuddered through her at the thought. Never in her life had she ever entertained the thought of going against her queen's wishes.

Her gaze slid to her left where Odson Blackridge stood to the other side of the doors. She hadn't seen the man in years.

Why was he here?

She turned her attention back to the far end of the room, where Jori stood facing the queen and her guard. They still hadn't moved.

The great doors swung closed and Kymri was moving forward. The second she started walking, Odson moved in a step behind.

They stopped, flanking Jori.

The queen blinked, shuttering the raw emotion away. Her gaze broke from Jori's face to Kymri and Odson behind him and back to Jori.

She straightened and turned to Kymri's mother, "My antechamber."

Kolina bowed her head, descending the dais toward Jori. The queen remained as she was while they were led away.

Jori pulled his shirt on, catching Kymri from the corner of his eye and stopped to pull her into his embrace. Her arms enveloped him.

Kolina stopped several paces ahead, "Come along."

Kymri couldn't read her mother's expression.

Jori twined his fingers with Kymri's and resumed walking. He didn't appear to have noticed Odson behind him with his escort of guards bringing up the rear.

She didn't know why Odson was walking with them, but what little she knew of him, she doubted he would have done so without good reason.

Kolina led them into the queen's antechamber, which was much less formal and more comfortable. The escort resumed their position to either side of the door. Jori turned then, as the door clicked shut, and he noticed Odson, the shock of his presence clear in his expression.

"Uncle Odson, what are you doing here?"

"Your father sent me to look for you."

"My father?"

Odson nodded, "After your last broadcast was never followed up on, he started calling the Coast Guard, and anyone else he could, to go out and find you. Even me." His mouth quirked at the corner.

"Shit," he breathed. "My dad called *you* and the Coast Guard?"

The door at the opposite end of the room opened, and the Queen's Guard filed through, followed by the speaker of the council and then the queen herself. She'd removed her assembly robes. As soon as she crossed the threshold, the door closed behind the queen. She walked up to Jori, looking up into his face, ignoring his linked hand with Kymri's.

Finally, her gaze fell to Kymri, "Have you told him?"

Which part?

She shook her head. None of it.

The queen's gaze then slid to Odson, the corner of her mouth rose, "Now I understand why you're here. You should have told me." Her expression shifted to immovable steel.

Odson cleared his throat and bowed his head, "I promised her I wouldn't."

The queen looked stung. She stepped back.

Kymri held her breath.

The queen returned her attention to Jori, and after several long moments, she seemed to accept Odson's reason.

She turned away from them then, moving to the decanter at the back of the room and poured from it into several tumblers. She brought two forward, handed them to Jori and Odson, then returned for the third. She didn't offer it to Kymri, "None for you," she said, with a finger pointed at her from over the glass before she knocked the drink back, swallowing hard.

Jori and Odson drank theirs and Kolina moved in to take the glasses away.

"It seems there is a long, interesting, story going on here that needs to be told," the queen said, gesturing toward chairs surrounding a table. The queen took the chair at the head of the table, Kolina and the speaker to either side. Kymri sat next to her mother and Jori moved in beside her. Odson took the chair across from her, drawing the full weight of her curiosity.

Indeed.

She was about to find out more about her lover than she had expected.

"He hasn't been initiated," the queen said.

Initiated? Her heart lodged in her throat.

Odson shook his head, his eyes on Jori.

She studied him for a long moment. No one spoke.

Kymri's impatience was about to bubble over.

The queen's gaze finally returned to Odson. "Tell me what you know."

Odson's mouth compressed under the steady gaze of the queen.

Jori stared just as hard.

"What the fuck is going on?"

Why did this queen react that way when she saw his mother's name tattooed on his chest? She'd instantly shut down the proceedings.

"And why the hell are you *here,* of all places?" he threw at Odson. The queen seemed to know him?

His father had called him, and the Coast Guard, to find him? What the hell? He and his father hadn't exchanged two words in years, and he called out the hounds to find him? He thought he'd forgotten he even had a son.

Why call Uncle Odson?

And initiated into what?

His thoughts were a tornado in his skull, bouncing hard against the back of his eyeballs.

His eyes slid to Kymri's profile beside him. What hadn't she told him yet?

He scrubbed both hands over his face and drew in a deep breath, letting it out slowly, trying to ease the beginnings of a serious headache.

Odson was watching him. He was mostly unreadable, but there was a flicker of compassion in his eyes.

Jori sat a little straighter.

This couldn't be good.

Odson drew in a breath, still hesitating.

Not good at all.

Odson looked at the queen, opened his mouth then shut it again, clearly not know where to start.

His eyes turned back to Jori. "I'm not just a family friend, Jori, we really are blood."

"But why-"

"It's complicated."

"Just fucking start somewhere," Jori snarled, his nerves fraying. Maybe he was in the grip of a solid delusion. He already thought he'd been seeing dragons. He was probably still stranded on the little island with is crashed plane, eyes blank and drool oozing from his mouth waiting for rescue, because none of anything that's happened since had made any fucking sense.

He had the feeling that it wasn't about to get any clearer, either.

Kymri's hand slid into his again, and his heart rate slowed at the contact. He gave her fingers a little squeeze of reassurance, turning to look at her lovely face. She was so beautiful. And her expression was so full of concern for him.

This really wasn't going to be good.

Odson seemed to have found his starting point. He turned his attention back to the queen. "As you know, Elora fulfilled her mission to establish alliances with the other paranormal communities nearby on the continent. That's where we met. We got to know each other at Black River, where I was working for the Brandt boys.

It was incredible meeting my sister for the first time—but that's another story, for another time." His eyes flicked to Jori. "She left, heading back here."

Jori was struggling to absorb Odson's words. Paranormal community?

"She never returned," Kolina said.

Odson shook his head, "Some weeks after she left, she showed up at my door looking like hell." He swallowed hard, keeping his eyes on the queen. "She'd been captured and force-mated until it took hold."

The queen snarled, rising from her seat, and began pacing.

Jori's heart had stopped. Force mated? Raped?

"Continue." the queen snapped.

"I don't know if they let her go, or if she escaped them. I just know she didn't want to come back here in case they followed her back."

The queen stopped pacing, her face blanching. "Why you?"

Odson straightened his shoulders. "During our time getting to know one another, I had told her I didn't prescribe to their ways. That's why I was at Black River in the first place."

The queen seemed to accept this.

"She asked me to help her find a place in the city. She refused to stay with me in case they came looking for her, and she wasn't wrong. They showed up within days after she left. I helped her get a job and a place in the city where she could blend in." He drew a breath then, his eyes returning to Jori, "She met your father there."

Unformed thoughts slithered down the back of his brain.

"They fell in love; the bond began threading."

"Do you know if she told him the truth?"

Odson shrugged, "Yeah. She asked me to come in case he freaked out."

"Freak out, why?" Jori asked.

"About what she was," Kymri whispered.

"And what you were going to be." Odson said to Jori.

What the fuck?

"Jonathan knew she was pregnant, he accepted that."

Jori blinked. *'...force-mated until it took hold.'* His stomach rolled over. Jonathan Mountainside wasn't his father. Some unknown rapist was. Was this why his relationship with him fell apart after his mother disappeared?

Jori's voice shook, "So you're telling me that he isn't my father? That my mother was raped by some sick fuck?"

Odson nodded.

Jori swallowed down the bile, his fists clenching hard. Kymri's grip on his hand tightened and he eased his grasp of her fingers.

"And the rest?" The queen prompted.

"We'd gone out of the city for this and found an abandoned campground."

"How did he handle it?"

Odson's mouth quirked at the corner, "Once he regained consciousness, it took a few minutes, but he otherwise handled it rather well, considering. She couldn't hold it long though, the pregnancy was taking a lot out of her, so she made me do it too."

"Do what?" Jori's voice erupted from his throat.

"Shift," Kymri said softly from beside him.

"Shift?" Jori's brain was a haze, he felt like he was lost in a cloud of marijuana smoke. "What does that mean?"

"Into dragon form."

Laughter burst from Jori's throat. The strain of the last few weeks finally snapping. "This isn't real. You guys are fucking shitting me," he laughed.

Odson sighed.

The queen bore an expression of patience, while the speaker and the others in the room looked on him with pity.

He reigned in his laughter and let his gaze finally turn to Kymri. She had a soft smile on her face. Raising their linked hands between them, she kissed his fingers, "We're not, Jori."

He dropped her hand. The chair he'd been sitting on scraped back across the floor as he jumped to his feet. "I've lost my fucking mind," he muttered. "All of this—all of it is fucking crazy."

Kymri slowly got to her feet, putting herself directly in front of him, so that he was forced to look down into her face. Into her eyes.

"Jori," she whispered, "it's real." She turned to the head of the table, "Your Majesty; may I? I'll bring him back, as I suspect there's more to this story that needs to be told."

"There is," Odson said.

The queen nodded.

"Come on, this won't take long," she said to Jori, linking her hand with his again and tugging him toward the door.

He let her.

"I saw dragons from my prison," he mumbled.

"Okay," she said.

Okay?

She led him back toward the courtyard he'd walked through before with his escorts between the main tower buildings and his prison. "You wait here." She pushed him to sit on a stone bench, then turned and walked to the center of the green space and began to undress.

What the hell was she doing? His body reacted to the sudden shift from what his brain was struggling to accept to the simplicity of physical desire. Her top dropped from her shoulders and there were no other thoughts. His cock jerked in his pants, and he was on his feet and moving toward her.

She waved a finger at him, "Sit." she stopped stripping until he did as she commanded.

His gaze slid around the large open space, wondering if anyone was watching them.

She kicked off the rest of her clothing and stepped back from the pile at her feet.

"Ready?"

Hell yeah, this was rational—well, stripping in the middle of a courtyard was far more rational than anything that had come out of the last hour. "Yes."

The space in front of Kymri wavered like old glass panes, obscuring his view of her glorious naked form. He blinked. Her hands moved to her abdomen. There was a swirl of air rushing and color wavering and making her shape look as though she were melting and reforming, growing.

He blinked again and a razor-toothed dragon towered over him in her place, large luminescent eyes focused on him.

His breath went out of him. Jesus fucking Christ.

Chapter 14

Kymri held her breath against the discomfort in her abdomen from the pressure of the encased child in her womb—and in lieu of Jori's reaction to her dragon form.

Slowly, she drew in a steady breath, inhaling him. He smelled of his own distinct musk that attracted her to him, the scent of the alcohol the queen had given him, and raw emotions. There was a little fear, quickly buried under excitement.

She could hear the shake of his breath and the pounding of his heart. He was on his feet, but he hadn't moved away from her, nor toward her.

"This isn't real," he whispered.

She huffed, her breath making the loose hairs around his face flutter. He sucked in a breath then.

"Kymri?"

She blinked, nudging a paw forward, drawing his attention to her claws. They were still hot pink.

His eyes went wide, "Fuck me," he whispered in awe.

In all their time alone on the beach, she'd never heard him swear so much as he had in the last quarter hour.

His hand was reaching out to her brightly colored claw. The subtle touch of his fingers drifting along the hard surface until he stepped closer, maintaining the contact. The rough skin of her paw, up along her arm until he connected with the scales that covered the rest of her.

She couldn't help purring at the feel of his touch moving over her body. His hand snapped away; eyes wide until he realized it wasn't a growl. Then he smiled, and her heart tilted. She loved his smile.

"Kymri, I don't know if I can believe this." He moved away so that he stood before her, looking up into her face. "Incredible. This is what the queen meant—if you'd told me yet."

Kymri let the magic go with a breath of relief. She hadn't expected to ever have to work at holding her form. "Part of it," she said, hands over her abdomen, his hands reaching out to steady her when she stumbled a couple of steps.

"Part?"

She nodded, "It's been getting harder to hold the magic to shift now…" she drew a deep, steadying breath, "now that I'm carrying your child." She looked up into his face.

She couldn't read it.

"You're pregnant?"

She nodded.

He drew in a shaky breath. "It's mine?"

She scowled, a little stung by the need for confirmation, but nodded, realizing he'd just found out that his father was not his biological father.

"I'm sorry, that was a dick thing to ask," he said as his hands came up to cup her face, his calloused thumb easing over the ridge of her scowl.

She caught his hand and drew it down to kiss the base of his thumb, "No matter. We need to return. The queen is waiting for us."

"She can wait a few more minutes. I haven't seen you since we last parted on the beach."

Now that she was in his proximity again, she could feel the heat of him through his clothes. She'd forgotten that she stood naked, apparently, he was well aware. He pulled her against him, his arousal hard against her belly. Turning her face up to his, the intensity of his gaze drank in her features before his lips descended over hers. He kissed her with such tender hunger, she could feel him wrapping around her heart, the final pieces of him sliding into place and she knew. She knew the threading of their bond was nearly complete.

Scooping up her clothes, he led her back to the stone bench, pulling her down to straddle him. Reaching between them, she unzipped his shorts and pulled him free, fingers sliding over the ridged length. Jori's hands grasped her face, tongue testing her lips. Sweeping her tongue against his, she lowered herself onto him with a sigh.

"God I've missed you," he whispered.

He throbbed inside her. Relaxing her muscles a fraction, she slid lower, eliciting gasps from both of them.

"I've missed you too."

Holding his face between her palms, her lips touched his again. His hands gripped her hips, encouraging her to move against him. As soon as she started to move, his hands roamed over her ribs, her back and her breasts, then locked her to him.

She rode him hard.

They came together, their breathing filled the stillness of the courtyard.

With extreme deliberation, Jori eased his hold on Kymri to help her dress before returning to the queen to face the rest of the story.

He knew he'd missed her during their time apart. Now that he had her back in his arms again, he knew with certainty they wouldn't be forcefully parted again. When his lips touched her again, he knew. Something slid into place within him.

And she was going to have his child. He felt like she'd thumped him right in the chest.

He looked at her, fastening the last of the straps of her ceremonial armor.

Was this what Jonathan felt when he looked at his mother? Knowing she was pregnant with someone else's kid?

He studied Kymri. If this child hadn't been his, would he feel the same?

Finished, she smiled up at him.

Hell yes.

He always knew how much his father loved his mother.

Now he understood it better.

This was for life.

He was just sorry that the relationship between himself and Jonathan Mountainside hadn't been able to withstand the loss of the one person that held them together.

He reached out a hand toward Kymri's belly. His fingers shook. Could he be as good a father as Jonathan had been before his mother disappeared?

Kymri closed the distance, taking his hand in hers and pressing his palm to her womb. He could feel the hard lump.

He searched her face. She was watching him closely.

"The child seems to have created a shell around itself to protect against the magic of the shift when I go into dragon form. Because we are connected, the energy is pulled from my reserve."

"Does it hurt you?"

She shook her head, linking her fingers through his, "We must go back," she began to walk back toward the door that would lead them back to the queen's antechamber and all those waiting for them.

He picked up his pace, inserting himself in front of her so that she walked into him.

There was so much he wanted to say but it was all lodged in his throat, so he pulled her into him and kissed her, trying to translate all of it in a way he could express.

When he finally released her lips, she stared up at him, eyes wide and full of unshed tears.

He kissed her eye lids and the tip of her nose.

They entered the antechamber hand in hand.

The queen looked at both of them, "Good."

The woman Kymri had been seated next to looked on them with a warm smile.

Odson wore an expression of deep relief and everyone else looked as though they wanted to get on with the discussion.

Odson took a moment to collect his thoughts to resume his story. "Once Jonathan got his bearings and was able to accept seeing both of us shift in and out of our dragon forms, he just went with it. I've never seen a human accept something so completely." Odson's attention turned back to Jori "Your father's a rare guy."

Jori nodded, not knowing what to say to that.

Odson went on, "I didn't stick around, just checked in now and then. When you were born, I couldn't tell who was more delighted at your arrival, they both doted on you so much." He smiled at the fond memory. "Elora always held a deep-seated tension in her. She never knew when and if they would find the two of you. She didn't talk much about it, but I could see it in her eyes, it was the same look that had ingrained itself when she'd come to me for help.

"Jonathan was concerned about all the trips she took you on, trying to teach you about your heritage without actually telling you the truth of it. She wasn't ready for that. As much as she desperately wanted you to know who you were, she was terrified to lose you to it, too."

"Why would she?" he asked.

"As much as males are not welcome here among the females, it's very different among the male tribes. They're prized, indoctrinated, and instilled with a belief in their superiority and their right to dominate and rule the weak. They believe it is their right to take any female they want to procreate with, and then take the male child to make themselves stronger." Odson sighed, looking tired. "It's a fucked-up system."

"Ours isn't perfect either," Kymri said, her voice low.

The queen's head snapped toward her; eyes narrowed.

The woman next to Kymri stood, putting herself in the queen's line of vision. "Your Majesty," she said softly, drawing her attention. "In her current state, my daughter is acutely aware she will have to make a hard decision when the child comes."

"I'm aware of the choices too, Kolina, we *all* have to make them for the continued safety of our people."

The woman named Kolina inclined her head and resumed her seat beside Kymri.

Odson's expression held compassion as he looked at Jori's woman and then to Jori. "You can't stay here, Jori. And she has to decide what to do with the child."

Jori's fists clenched.

The queen spoke, her voice strong and absolute, "Males are not welcome to live on this island for a reason. There has been far too much strife, and attempts to dominate and subjugate in the past."

Odson's nod confirmed it, "They will come for you as soon as they know where you are, Jori."

Jori blinked.

Kymri's hand tightened on his.

A fissure fizzled in his brain as the realization of everything they were saying began to work its way into his consciousness. *They* weren't just dragon shifters. His mother had been, and she had been impregnated by one. That made *him* one too.

Jesus fuck, I'm a goddamned dragon?

He felt as though a layer of frost was creeping up his spine as he recalled the battle between the large dragon and the two smaller ones outside his prison walls.

He looked around at the faces of the woman gathered in the room.

Kymri.

The queen.

The Queen's Guard.

No wonder they were armed.

And that dragon now knew where they were.

"Odson, how did you find me?" Ice was sliding through his chest.

"Your video broadcast gave your coordinates."

Jori's eyes flicked to the queen. Her expression unreadable.

It wasn't just regular people this island was being protected from.

No fucking wonder Kymri had pulled a knife on him and was willing to cut him for some batteries.

Their lives really were at risk, should others find out who and where they were.

He jumped to his feet.

He fucked up.

He paced away from the table toward the wall needing to gather his thoughts.

He thought his mother was teaching him so that he could share the legends with the rest of the world. She was teaching him so that he could understand something of himself, without telling him all of it. Still protecting her people.

Jori turned toward the queen, "This is the reason for the assembly. Why I'm here."

She inclined her head.

He put his fists on the table, leaning forward, head bowed. He finally looked up at Odson, "That's how you found me. I've been Vlogging and streaming for a long time now. How can they have made the connection between me and the certainty of this place?"

"Jori." The older man shrugged, his gaze flicked between him and the queen. "They believe you're an infiltrator for the male tribe."

"It's become quite obvious he didn't have full knowledge before now. But that doesn't mean they weren't using him without his knowledge," Kolina said.

Jori's heart dropped into his stomach.

How could they know? How could they know to make that connection?

Jori looked up at Odson, "What do you know of my mother's disappearance?"

Chapter 15

Anger rolled off of Jori's body in hot waves. Kymri could feel it radiating around her.

His whole world was turned upside down.

She watched Odson Blackridge as he answered Jori's question.

"Not much. Not anything more than your father knew to tell me when she disappeared."

"When did this happen?" Kolina asked.

"About 20 years ago." Jori said.

"You should have come to us." The queen's voice carried down the table despite her soft tone.

"With all due respect, your Majesty, as far as Elora's wishes, you were all to have believed she'd disappeared long before that. I would not have been believed and likely would have been shut away as a traitor and a spy." His gaze slid back to Jori.

"She disappeared when I was in my teens. Why then, why now?" Jori said.

"They know where we are now; we need to prepare. Three attacked us this time and we almost lost Zayli. We have to be ready for when they return, and if there are more next time," Kymri said. "We've relied on the magnetic fields created around this place by the ley lines to shield us for a very long time. We knew it couldn't last forever. You know we will protect you to the death."

"None of you should have to, Kymri Steelscale."

"*They* make it so that we have to," she said softly. "None of us wish to exist under that kind of servitude, and none of us will allow our queen to submit herself to such degradation either."

"Your Majesty," Kolina drew her attention, "Allow Kymri and I to go to Black River and speak to the Brandt family, they may have connections to help us."

Odson said "There are some government officials in intelligence, friendly to the family. They may be able to help locate a general direction of their lair using satellite surveillance. If the family is reluctant to get involved, I'll approach the individuals myself. I've interacted with them at the bar for paranormals."

"Your majesty, if I may go too, I'd like to try to fix the mess I made with my broadcasts. Once outside the ley line grid I can send out another broadcast informing the world I am alive and well, to stop looking for me and let them all know there's nothing to be found here."

The queen looked at him long and hard, "You came all the way out here to prove our existence. Why should I believe that you wouldn't take this opportunity to exploit us and make your fortune?"

Jori shifted, an expression of guilt drawing his features.

"I'll go with them."

The queen's gaze slid to Kymri; she could feel the weight of her assessment. After a long moment she said, "Kolina, I need you here. Marli will travel with Kymri and Odson to speak to the government contacts."

Relief tumbled through Kymri's insides. Marli was safe.

The queen went on, "She has seen our attackers in their human form; she can identify them if needed. Jori will make his announcement. Kymri, if he tries to betray us, your orders are to kill him before he can. No matter your relationship. Our people's lives are at risk."

Nausea rolled through Kymri. She nodded, not daring to look at Jori.

"Your Majesty—" Odson's voice was low.

"Those are her orders." The queen's words cut through his growl. "Dismissed."

Kymri and Jori shifted to leave, but Odson didn't move. "Your Majesty." His low voice pulled everyone's attention. "Initiate him."

Kymri gasped, as did several others, all attention suddenly on the queen.

"No."

"He'd be vulnerable if we're attacked."

"No."

Odson's jaw tightened, his fists curling in to stop the stream of curses she could sense he held back.

Kymri spared a glance in Jori's direction. His expression was unreadable, his posture incredibly tense.

"Dismissed."

No one waited to be told a third time.

Out in the hall, Kolina approached Kymri, "Before you leave, I will meet with all of you."

Kymri nodded.

Odson cast Kolina a glance.

"Timing, Odson," Kolina said.

The older man snarled and stalked away.

Kymri studied her mother's face and dropped her voice, "Do you think she'll do it?"

Kolina's eyes followed Odson as he and Jori disappeared down the corridor. "Maybe."

Excitement spiked in Kymri, but she tried to keep it under control. "Don't get too excited daughter. He has to prove himself unswervingly loyal before she'll ever consider initiating him, especially here. Otherwise, there'd have to be a major disaster that would make her desperate enough to put herself at such a high risk."

"He wouldn't harm her."

"No, I don't think he would. Not willingly. That's the key, isn't it? He didn't willingly lead those three males here either, did he?"

"How could he have known?"

"There's too much he doesn't know. But he knows just enough to be dangerous to us and to himself." She sighed and reached out a hand to Kymri, letting her fingers gently squeeze her arm. Kymri had never seen her look so weary. "If he's not as you think—if you have any sense—he may betray us, you *will* have to silence him. Go to Black River, make contact with the continental intelligence officers, and find out what you can about our enemies. Come back to us, have your child, and return to duty if that is your wish. I will help raise the youngling. If Jori's smart, he'll return to his life and forget about us."

"And what of the attackers? Odson is right about his vulnerability if they go after him. If he can shift, he can defend himself. He can help us defend our island."

"Would he?"

"Why wouldn't he?" she countered.

"Say he did. Then what? A large male on this island of females. What makes you think he wouldn't just exert dominance for himself?"

"That's not who he is."

"And you know this? In the short amount of time you've been with him, you've had these long in-depth conversations between rounds of mating?"

Kymri's cheeks flamed, "I know this. This journey of his was all about connecting with his mother because he loved her so much. He wouldn't destroy something so important to her."

Kolina snorted, "When did you become so sentimental?" When Kymri didn't answer, she said "I'll meet with you in an hour, prepare yourselves to leave." Her expression softened, "Marli arrived here with Odson; she's waiting to see you."

Kymri watched her walk away.

Was she being sentimental?

She felt deep inside herself that she was right about Jori. But her mother's words tugged at the dutiful warrior in her.

It was her life's duty to protect her queen and her people. She didn't have room for sentimentality.

She couldn't allow herself to be blinded. There was too much at risk.

And Marli was back. Her heart lightened as she rushed back toward the residential section of the compound.

Jori's mind was a whirlwind of thought as he made his way back to his prison to retrieve what little he had with him. Odson walked beside him, just as silent.

When they reached the prison, Odson grunted. "Not a bad prison, if I recall. I've been in worse since." He mumbled.

They waited for Kymri and another woman called Marli in the open courtyard, who both appeared in jeans, shirts, and solid boots, carrying backpacks. He wondered how many illegal weapons they had hidden.

Kymri didn't speak to him. She seemed more distant.

She had orders to kill him if he even thought about exposing them.

His chest tightened. Had he lost her trust? He couldn't blame her—any of them.

He had to make it right.

He clung to that thought above all else. Above everything he'd just learned about his mother, these people and himself. It was a surreal.

He had to make things right with Kymri—for Kymri. If he didn't, she was in danger. He couldn't bear the thought of being responsible for putting her in danger, or anyone else on the island. No one spoke to each other as they waited for Kolina.

Jori watched Kymri across the distance between them. She stood, back straight, her expression set. He wanted to pull her into his arms and make her melt into him again. He missed that. He missed the feel of her in his arms, liquid against him. He wanted that again. They'd had paradise for a short while.

"You'll sail out to meet with the Coast Guard waiting outside the barrier. Odson, you have transportation to get yourselves to Black River?"

At his nod, she continued, "As soon as you have the information you need, get back here as fast as possible," she said to Kymri and Marli. "Odson, the queen thanks you for your help. Jori Mountainside—" she said his name, but nothing else seemed to come from her open lips as she looked into his face, studying him, several emotions flitting across her features. She closed her mouth, left it at that. She then turned to her daughter and squeezed her hand, which elicited a look of surprise from Kymri, before she turned and left.

Marli led the way back along the path twisting down toward the harbor and the waiting ship.

Once aboard the sailing vessel, which was essentially a tall ship, Jori heard Marli speaking softly to Kymri, "I don't like leaving them like this. They need the guard at full capacity."

"I don't either. We should be helping to prepare the defenses against more attacks."

"If they come back with more than three..."

"I know."

In open waters, they met with the Coast Guard, where they changed ships. As soon as they were underway toward the coast, Jori asked a crew member about equipment to make a broadcast. He was offered a cell phone and the use of the computer in the mess hall. The engines were still gearing up as he made his short video reporting a freak storm, crash landing on an island and being rescued by a beautiful island girl, then followed the crew member to upload it to his Vlog. Hopefully this would help deter folks. Humans at least. He couldn't do anything about the male dragons now, it was too late for that. Maybe the rest of the world would remain oblivious.

Returning to join the others on deck, he found them talking to another man in civilian clothing, with hunched shoulders. Now he was sure he was delusional.

"Dad?"

Naked emotion flittered across the older man's haggard features as Jori walked toward them. His father pulled him into his embrace, making him feel ten years old again. Swallowing hard, he hugged his father back. After a long moment, Jonathan Mountainside released his son.

"Dad, what are you doing here?"

"I told you he called the Coast Guard," Odson grumbled.

"This was a close as anyone would allow me to get until you were found." Despite the relief shining through, Jonathan's face was tired, drawn, and uncharacteristically unshaven. His gaze turned toward Kymri and Marli, "Despite my hopes you never would, Odson said you found what you were looking for?"

Jori nodded.

"We need to talk."

"I need to call an old friend," Odson said, turning away from them toward Kymri and Marli, who followed suit.

"I can't believe you left your office to venture out on a Coast Guard ship, Dad."

Jonathan looked stung by the comment, "Jori, despite my limitations, you're everything to me."

His words hit Jori in the chest. When he responded, his voice was husky, "I uh... I thought I was a disappointment to you."

Jonathan grunted, "No, you're not. I was trying to steer you on a path that would keep you safe. And clearly I failed in that one thing your mother asked me to do."

"What do you mean?"

"She asked me to keep you safe from them. She was terrified they would find you and take you back with them."

Jori stared at his father, "The... male tribe?"

Jonathan nodded. Tears gathered in his eyes, "It was the last thing she made me promise her when she disappeared."

"You thought by keeping me tied to the campus, they wouldn't find me?"

It had been a good idea; he'd have blended in among all the thousands of students and faculty in the middle of a city of millions.

Jori put his hand on his father's shoulder and squeezed, blowing out his breath. It explained a lot. Jonathan's frustration when Jori pushed harder to go in other directions. It wasn't Jonathan shutting down the relationship, now that he looked back with a different lens. Jori was the one putting distance between them.

Except when it came to talking about his mother. Jori had tried to talk about her with his father, and Jonathan did shut down the topic.

"Dad, what happened when mom disappeared?"

The expression on Jonathan's face when he looked at Jori twisted his gut.

It was something he clearly still didn't want to talk about. And for a long moment, Jori feared Jonathan would shut down the conversation again.

"She was taken, again."

Chapter 16

I t had been a long time since Kymri was in a car, and she remembered why she disliked them. They were confining. At least she wasn't tall like Jori. Despite the shorter length of her legs, she still found she couldn't get comfortable during the endless drive to Black River. She'd rather be flying. Glancing at Marli, she could see she felt the same. ***

Odson was behind the wheel of what Jori had mumbled was a 'classic Mustang Shelby' before getting in the front passenger seat.

Seated behind Odson, Kymri could see Jori's profile when he turned his head away from the window. His gaze had been focused out of the side window most of the drive. Worry gnawed at her. The pressures of discovering the reality of her world, their child, the attacks, and now there was something more. Something Jonathan Mountainside had told him when they were alone aboard the Coast Guard ship.

He was in shock. She could feel it in the way he distanced himself from everyone in the wake of that conversation. Odson kept at him with concern and had gone to find out from Jonathan what had happened. Neither of the Mountainside men were saying anymore. Jonathan told Jori he would remain in Charleston rather than return home.

As the car wound its way through the mountains, Kymri hoped Jori would tell her what was troubling him. She ached to see him so... so burdened. The others felt it too; no one talked more than was necessary. Whatever it was, was heavy.

For now, they drove.

Odson's contact was going to meet them at Black River. Apparently, he was on vacation with his companion and was willing to do this favor for Odson.

On reaching Black River, they went straight up to the Brandt house.

"Who are these people?" Jori whispered to Odson.

"Bear shifter family in charge of this territory. They're a hub for paranormals, whether they like it or not. I work for one of the Brandt boys. Good folks."

Jori climbed the steps, shaking his head. "Bear shifters and paranormals. Right." He sighed.

Heidi Brandt, the family matriarch, welcomed them into her home. Everyone else was out working for the day. After paying their respects and explaining the situation over a pot of coffee, Heidi Brandt invited them to stay as long as they needed.

Kymri liked the older woman. She reminded her of Marli's mother, warm and welcoming with a deep sense of caring for others. They said their good-byes over a lump in Kymri's throat.

Heidi Brandt tugged at something in her. As much as she shut out any need for family ties, Mrs. Brandt's maternal aura picked at the thread of need, encouraging the shroud around her to unravel a little. A need Kolina hadn't been able to fulfill in Kymri, that Kymri resolved wouldn't have a place in her life. But she wasn't her mother and as much as she buried that need, it was still there.

Her hand slid over her belly. Maybe she could make things different? She could at least try. She glanced at Jori's tired face. She realized she wanted it all. She wanted to continue her duties as a guardian of her home, have a warm relationship with her child, and keep Jori in her life. It was the kind of life she saw when she looked at Heidi Brandt, as they passed the family photos adorning the walls of her house on their way back out to Odson's car.

Heidi Brandt squeezed Kymri's hand and smiled at her, "It was so lovely to meet you Kymri Steelscale; I hope to see you again." She turned to Odson, "Come up to see us more often."

Odson nodded, "Will do, ma'am."

"Jori," she said, approaching him with her hands reaching up to his face, "you look so much like your mother. When I met her, she had so much hope for you. Even before you were born, she loved you fiercely."

Kymri's heart ached at the naked vulnerability in his face as he struggled to control his emotions. He smiled weakly as Mrs. Brandt patted his cheek.

"You and Kymri come back to see us too. Anytime." She spoke briefly to Marli as Kymri got into Odson's car.

As soon as Marli joined them, they were on their way toward town and Blaine Brandt's paranormal club, where Odson worked.

"We're going to meet my guy at the club," Odson said, steering the car along a narrow dirt road. "I already reached out to my contact with the dragons at a nearby camp. They've seen three unknown males in the area."

"There were three that followed me, they're probably the same males."

"I missed you while you were gone. What happened?" Kymri asked Marli.

"The bastards spotted me while on patrol, and followed me to a hedonist beach where I lost them. I didn't want to lead them back to the island, so I stowed away and came here, where I met up with Odson." Marli cracked her window. "Lucky for me, he was already packed and about to leave to go looking for your man here, so I hitched a ride with him."

Marli was still looking at Kymri when she broke into a grin.

"What?"

"Launia told me you're carrying a youngling."

Kymri grimaced, "Yeah, would seem so."

"That's so great! I can't wait to be an aunty, I'm going to spoil that kid so much!" she laughed reaching over to hug Kymri, who couldn't help but laugh at Marli's delight.

"So, at this camp you mentioned, Odson, males and females live there peacefully?" Kymri asked.

"Pretty much - as peacefully as any other community, I suppose." He navigated around a large pothole, "Not everyone tries to dominate those around them."

Kymri watched the trees on the way.

"Yeah sure," Marli snorted.

Kymri turned away from her window to see Jori watching her. She couldn't read his expression. He turned back toward the windshield without a word.

L ittle more was said amongst the foursome during the rest of the car ride to town where Odson lived and worked.

Communities of paranormals.

He never would have dreamed they existed before his first sighting of a real dragon. He could only imagine what 'paranormals' meant. Did he really want to know? He'd always thought he was an open-minded guy. This was beyond that.

This is what he thought he was chasing all these years, not really thinking any of it truly was real. Myths, legends, stories.

And yet, 'paranormals' apparently didn't just live in remote areas and lost islands. They were right here among everyone else.

Kymri, his island beauty. Dragon with hot pink claws. Mother of his child.

Life had taken a sudden hard left turn when he took off in his mother's Cessna. He crashed into a whole other reality. He wondered again if maybe he had lost his mind and was dead or delirious on the beach.

The crash flashed through his mind. He'd seen a woman in the plane. He'd been moved from his seat to the back... where he'd later made love to Kymri for the first time. Was that first memory real or a dream? Had it been her? All this time?

Their meeting, their tentative friendship, their budding romance and then the sky falling down on him and discovering the legend of the dragons was real, not just real, that they were people and his mother was one of them.

This was so fucked up.

He stared at the passing trees lining the road winding through the mountains. He was so fucked up.

His father's words steam rolled over everything else. They had elicited so much turmoil in him he couldn't speak beyond, "Why didn't you tell me this before?"

It was all he could say, again and again. The shock had hit him so hard, and he could see how much it pained Jonathan.

It ripped into his father to have kept this secret from him—that there was nothing he could do about it. It wasn't a secret he'd ever wanted to keep but held it alone for all of these years while they both grieved the loss of her.

All through their meeting with Mrs. Brandt, she reminded him of Elora in so many ways. He was in a fog.

He needed time to process it. All of it. But there wasn't time.

Dusk fell as they drove along the winding tree-lined roads to town. It was fully dark when they parked the car outside a club that was already lit up, with patrons lined up at the door. Odson brought them in through the back where the bass of the music beat through the walls and along the floors of offices and kitchens at the back of the building.

"Through here," Odson said, pulling open a door to music and flashing lights which assaulted their senses.

The place was already full. The hair on his nape rose. He'd spent enough time in clubs to know this one was different. The atmosphere was charged. Odson was unfazed; he worked here, this was natural for him. Kymri and Marli, however, were on their guard.

Odson approached a broad-shouldered man seated at the bar who turned and stood, greeted Odson with a friendly hug, and introduced a petite woman beside him.

Jori glanced back to Kymri, who remained close to him, noting that Marli was no longer with her.

Odson spoke to the guy behind the bar who nodded and waved him back toward the door they'd just come through. "Come on," he said over the pounding music, leading them and the new couple back toward the office area.

As soon as they were in the quieter space, Odson introduced them all. "Jori Mountainside, Kymri Steelscale, this is Agent Carson Perenga and Lirikai. Carson's an old friend, works for the GPSA. Where's Marli?"

"She's looking around the club, she'll be back in a minute," Kymri said.

"GPSA?" Jori asked.

"Global Paranormal Security Agency." Odson answered.

"I see," Jori said adding yet another tick to the 'weird things to remember' list.

Odson turned to Carson, "Remember that island in the middle of the Atlantic?"

Carson nodded, "Trouble?"

"Yeah."

"What do they need?"

"Intel if you can get it? Three dragon males attacked the island. I want to know where they came from."

"I'll see what I can get from satellites."

Odson nodded, "Thanks."

Carson grinned, "Boss sends his love."

Odson snorted, "Sly bastard owes me a fresh round of cards."

The agent stepped forward, linking his fingers through Lirikai's, "I'll get back to you as soon as I can."

"On behalf of my queen and our people, thank you," Kymri said.

"I remember her, before your people moved to the archipelago," he said to Kymri. He smiled at Lirikai, brushing his lips across her fingers, "You'd like her."

Jori extended his hand to Perenga, "Thanks, man."

Perenga studied him a moment, "You're the internet celebrity that went missing in the Bermuda Triangle. I've seen your show—it's good. Too bad it got complicated for you." He grinned.

"Yeah, well, who'd have thought this shit was real?"

Carson laughed, "You have no idea, man, no idea," he said, dropping his gaze to Lirikai again.

"Are you both, ah—dragons, too?"

Carson shrugged, "A dragon, yes, but not like this guy," he said clapping a hand on Odson's shoulder.

"I am Barra'kidai," Lirikai said.

"Interesting," he said, as though he had an idea what a Barra'kidai might be.

She chuckled, "Barracuda."

Jori managed to not jump out of his skin when long jagged teeth descended from her pretty mouth.

Carson laughed again, "Good luck, man."

Kymri and Jori followed as Lirikai led Carson out of the room.

Jori noticed the awe on Kymri's face.

"A Barra'kidai," she breathed.

Seriously, was his dragon woman fan-girling right now?

He shrugged when she turned her gaze up to him.

"Now *she* is a legend."

Chapter 17

"I'll be right back," Marli said to Kymri.

"Where are you going?"

She was already moving away and didn't bother shouting back over her shoulder. Dancers closed around as she moved through the space. Marli would have been tempted to lose herself among them if it weren't for the glimpse of a familiar face by the bar. By the time she reached it, he was gone, and she turned to see where to. Her backpack was in the trunk of Odson's car, but that didn't mean she was defenseless. She did have to be careful, though. This was a paranormal space for all sorts, and while she was a dragon—top of the food chain, as far as she was concerned—that didn't mean other types weren't a threat. She'd gone nearly full circle by the time she homed in on him, confirming her suspicion.

Dragonsdammit, he was here.

The fine hairs on her body rose.

This place was a neutral zone and she'd promised Odson to maintain the peace within the walls.

Where were his two buddies? Why was he here? Was it coincidence?

Marli didn't believe in coincidences.

Three male dragons here. And if things went sideways, she doubted a single individual in this place would help.

They were on their own.

She squeezed her way back through the crowd toward the offices where she'd left Kymri and the others. "Where is everyone?" she demanded of Odson.

"What's wrong?"

"They're here."

"Shit. Jori and Kymri went for a walk; they needed to talk. Carson and Lirikai took off to get the Intel we asked for."

"The leader is in the club; I couldn't see his wingmen."

"Show me. I want to see his face. We'll figure out a way to take them down later."

Marli led him back out to the crowded space. He was nowhere to be found." She turned to Odson shaking her head. He pointed toward the door and they made their way out.

The outside air was frigid on her skin compared to the close confines of the club. The streets were empty save for a solitary figure leaning on Odson's car parked under a flickering lamp.

Odson barreled in his direction, Marli close behind, nearly running into him when he stopped short.

"Stenlen."

"Old man." He grinned. He inhaled deeply through his nose; his gaze fixed on Marli. "Ah, I've been looking for you."

"This him?"

She nodded in answer.

"What are you doing here?"

"Looking for you, of course," He held up his hands, stepping away from the car toward Odson. "Why else would I come to a nowhere shit hole like this?"

"What do you want?"

"A piece of *that* to start," he turned his grin on Marli, "and a bit of a chat. That's all."

"Right."

"Honest."

"Talk."

Stenlen sighed, "So blunt. My boss sent me to work things out. We know where your island is now. We can take it anytime we want."

Marli snorted, he ignored her.

"And our Heir."

"What does that have to do with us?" Marli snapped.

He shrugged but didn't elaborate.

"It means they'll be more openly aggressive," Odson said.

Marli glanced at him, his face drawn. This wasn't good. Fear rippled down her back. If Odson was worried about this, it was serious.

"Yeah, thanks for that, Old Man. You brought him right to us, made things a whole lot easier."

"Son of a bitch!" Odson exploded.

Marli could feel his magic shimmer, "Don't—not here!" she shouted, as Stenlen dropped into a defensive position, preparing to shift. "You'll destroy the town." She held her breath as Odson reined himself in.

Oh, this is bad. Very bad.

She needed to find Kymri.

Kymri and Jori watched Carson and Lirikai drive away in his jeep, leaving them alone in the back alley.

Alone.

Jori slid his fingers along her palm. Hers curled over his and he pulled her to him. It felt so good to be in his arms again. Her heart thumped as he looked at her parted lips. He kissed her with all the gentleness and longing of an absent lover. She was nearly lost, melting into him.

Her hands slid around his torso, pulling his shirt up so she could slide her hands over this skin. Her tongue swept over his, pressing her body to his so that he backed up to the wall behind him.

His hands wandered down her back to grip her bottom, pulling her against him. He was hard and ready for her. He felt amazing and she couldn't get close enough to him.

Reluctantly freeing her lips, he sighed and rested his forehead on hers.

"Jori?" Her voice was soft as her fingers reached up to his cheek. He'd been so distant since they left the coast. Troubled and agitated.

He swallowed hard. "She's alive—my mother. All this time."

Kymri leaned back to see his face. "Elora's alive? But why...?"

"They have her."

Her heart stopped. She watched the minute expressions shift across his face as she processed the meaning of his words.

"My father—" he cleared his throat over the lump growing in it. He started again, "Dad told me she made him promise to keep her secret for my sake—my safety."

They would have come for him, if they knew he was a dragon.

She nodded. "She's in their lair?"

He released her and scrubbed a hand over his face. "Possibly. He didn't know for sure." He walked away from her a few feet and turned back. His face was twisted, "Jesus, Kymri, it nearly destroyed him to finally tell me the truth. I haven't seen him like that since she—since she disappeared."

"Does Odson know?"

Jori shook his head, "Mom explicitly told Dad never to let him know the truth. He'd end up dead."

Kymri reached for Jori's hand. The contact seemed to give him focus, and he calmed. "She was right. He would. Knowing him, he'd go after her."

"I doubted him, Kymri. I thought my dad didn't want me around all this time. I don't know how he could have kept a secret like that and done nothing."

Jori's eyes were haunted as he looked at her, Jonathan's truth naked in them.

"He did what he had to in order to protect you."

"I'm not even his blood."

"You're his son. That was clear on the Coast Guard boat. Very clear."

No wonder he'd been so distant since they left the coast.

"He said she was going back to the island to ask the queen for permission to return with us. And that she was going to ask the queen to initiate me. I was of age." He drew a deep breath. "And then she called him, told him to keep me safe and that it was important they never find out about me."

"Never?"

He shook his head.

Usually they were frantic to find the male dragonlings as children, to do the initiation themselves to establish dominance and loyalty. They lost some interest once that time passed. There was less value, less effort, put into finding the offspring. Unless they were important. Very important.

"Jori, did your mother tell your father who your sire was?" Kymri's heart began to hammer in her chest as her stomach dropped.

"No, but Dad said she was terrified they'd find me."

It couldn't be what she was thinking. It just couldn't.

And yet, Elora was going to ask the queen to initiate him, rather than just do it herself, or ask Odson to do it.

The queen might have decided to have him executed instead.

Kymri's breath stalled. She still might.

"Jori, you can't go home with me."

"I know, you said I wouldn't be welcome."

"They'd very likely kill you."

"Why?"

"Because you're their enemy," a voice said.

Kymri whirled around. They were so focused on their discussion; she hadn't heard anything else. She hadn't heard the approach of the two men blocking the mouth of the alley. One looked like a boxer who lost a lot of fights, the other was so average her eyes nearly slid right past him.

"Who the hell are you?" Jori demanded.

"Friends, lad. Just friends come to take you home."

"Fuck." Kymri said, gaining a startled glance from Jori. One of the men took a step forward and she darted between him and Jori with a snarl. "Get back."

She called on her magic, preparing to shift.

"Oh no, you don't," the other male said, running forward faster than she could gather her magic. An iron circlet closed over her left wrist as the other male enclosed her right with its match.

She groaned with strain as her magic dissipated. "Jori, run," she panted.

"Too late for that, lass."

The last thing she saw was the heel of a heavy boot before her world went dark.

"**K**ymri!" Jori roared, "Don't you fucking touch her."

"Come on now, lad, just stay calm, it's best for all of us if you just come along."

"Fuck you," he spat, bringing his fists up as he stepped closer to Kymri's inert form on the damp ground.

"How sweet, he's defending his little dragoness," the other said, "She must be a good rut."

"Be careful, lad, you're going to get yourself hurt."

Jori's fist swung, connecting with the jaw of the man reaching for Kymri. "I told you not to fucking touch her."

The man straightened and grinned. "He's got spunk. His sire will like that."

"Hmm, he's going to be trouble, more like."

"Just knock his head, we don't have time to dick around."

"Agreed. Sorry, lad."

Jori felt the full impact of the back of a meaty fist, then the solid bricks of the wall behind him. Then nothing.

First, the sense of having been hit by a truck overwhelmed him. Pain throbbed in most of his body as it rocked and bounced.

They were in a vehicle.

He cracked his eyes open and his head swam as he tried to focus on his surroundings. Kymri sat with her back against the inside of the van wall, watching him. An ugly bruise was blossoming across the side of her face.

"I'm going to kill that motherfucker," he said, but it came out more like a wheezing groan.

Her smile was weak as she leaned to help him sit up. Determined to get vertical he resisted the urge to flop back to the floor of the van. "I've been in quite a few scraps in my time, but I've never been taken down by a backhander like that."

"If he were human, you wouldn't have been."

Jori chuckled, "Thanks for the ego stroke."

Kymri reached out and linked her fingers through his, bringing his hand to her lips. Her eyes were trained on his. "Things are going to get messy, Jori."

Her serious tone rolled through his body, "I know."

"You're going to have some decisions to make. You should take this time to think about what's important to you. Really important, because that will be tested very soon."

He looked down at the thick iron bands on her wrists, "They stop you from shifting?"

She nodded.

Then she couldn't escape. He remembered what was said before about probabilities for the destiny of female dragons, when they were discussed back in the queen's chamber. Had Elora been shackled to prevent her escape too?

He swallowed hard. Thoughts of his mother living like that wrenched his insides as he stared at Kymri. If that was his mother's fate, it likely would be hers too. He wouldn't let that happen.

He looked around the cabin of the van for something to try to pry the iron apart - a screwdriver, anything. There was nothing. Just an empty space. Unlinking their fingers, he reached for the cuff, inspecting it for a slip lock.

"What weapons do you have hidden on you?"

"They took them from me. Besides, you won't be able to open it," she said. "Only their king will be able to. He created them, he holds the power to open them, and from what my understanding is, he never does once they're locked in place."

"Bullshit, there has to be a key of some kind."

She shrugged, "Maybe. Maybe not." She sat calmly, her hands resting one atop the other over her lower belly. She wore the same expression he recognized from their earliest meetings on the island. That nearly unreadable expression when she was still deciding whether she was going to kill him or not.

Anger rose in him fierce and hot, "Why are you so damned calm? We have to get out of here."

"They won't hurt you."

"So? Doesn't mean I want to go with them; they're freaks."

A brow rose as she considered him.

"Not because they turn into dragons, dammit, because of their fucked-up way of thinking. No one deserves dominance over another."

"Do you *really* believe that? *Really*?"

"Of course, I do, why the hell would you ask me that?"

"Because when they initiate you, you're going to have to make some decisions."

"There's nothing to decide," he growled, "we'll find my mother and do whatever the hell we have to in order to get home."

She smiled at him. He didn't notice the gathering tears right away.

"What is it?"

"I love that about you."

His mouth dropped open as the air went out of his gut. He swallowed, trying to find the right time to inhale again. He reached for her, pulling her into his arms, cradling her in his lap. His hands cupped her face, his thumbs stroking the skin between her lower lip and chin before he kissed her with all the tenderness in his entire body. "I won't let them lock you away," he whispered. "I love you."

She searched his face for a long moment, "Bite my lip," she said.

"What?"

"You heard me; bite me."

He told her he loved her, and she responds with 'bite me'? What the hell? He-

"Ow!" Sharp pain stung his lower lip and he tasted blood.

"Bite me, dragonsdammit!" she said, and licked the blood from his lip.

He ought to have been revolted, but he realized he really wasn't.

A gleam shimmered in her eyes as they both felt his arousal against her thigh, seated as intimately as they were. The tip of her tongue darted out over her lower lip and retreated before he sank his teeth into it causing her to grunt against his sharp teeth. He released her instantly, the tang of her blood sweeping into his mouth with her tongue. A growl rumbled deep in his chest his hand gripped the back of her head to take control of her mouth. She tugged back against his hand and he released her instantly. The urge to dominate her had been right up front.

With forced gentleness, he reached for her again. He could feel her gaze on his face, reading him, judging him.

"Like I said, Jori, you will have some decisions to make." She leaned into him, the tip of her tongue sweeping away the last of the blood from his lip and kissed him softly. "I love you too, Jori Mountainside. I just hope it's enough. For both of us."

Chapter 18

The brakes squealed as the van halted, causing Kymri to jerk into Jori.

He grabbed her and kissed her as the engine was cut, licking away the remnants of blood from her lips as she'd done for him.

She was his. He was hers. The threading of their bond was sealed.

Would it be enough?

She hoped so with every part of her being.

If it wasn't... Well, if it wasn't... She would have to do what was needed to protect her people. No matter the consequences to herself. And her child.

Her hands slid over his bearded face. This could be the last time she would feel the silky thick bristles beneath her fingers. Her cheek slid along his, inhaling the scent of him. She planted a kiss between his thick brows, then one last one on his full lips and disengaged herself from his lap, sorry for the instant loss of the warmth of his body against hers.

The van rocked then two doors slammed a moment before the back doors were thrown open to reveal the two thugs from the alley. A third stepped into view, grinning at them, "Well, it's about bloody time."

Jori reached for her hand.

"They tell me you don't like Clive here," he said with a laugh. His gaze shifted from Jori to Kymri. He nodded with grudging approval, "Could do worse," his eyes shot back to Jori, "Could do better."

There was a barely audible growl rumbling low. It was coming from Jori.

There it was.

The male dragon chuckled.

Kymri could feel her own dragon paying attention.

"Your sire will be pleased to see you."

Jori remained silent.

"I don't think he's all that interested in your king," Kymri said. She felt the slight clench of his hand around hers.

"Oh, he will be," his eyes gleamed with maliciousness, "especially when he meets the king's consort."

If she'd been human, Jori's hand would have crushed hers. He seemed to realize how hard he was squeezing, and his fist jerked open, releasing her.

"Really? Anyone I know? I would love to meet a woman that could stand to be around a king for longer than a few hours. Unless of course, she's being inspired to stick around," she said holding up her shackles and giving her wrists a little wriggle.

"Shut it," the thug called Clive snapped at her, stepping toward her.

The talkative guy held up a hand. "You left that mark on her face?"

"Stenlen, she was being difficult."

Stenlen sighed. "Merwin, explain to Clive again why we don't hit the dragon ladies."

"Makes them difficult," Merwin said.

"Great, now that's explained, shall we go?" He gestured forward, sweeping his hand toward the exterior of the van, and moving aside to make room for them to exit.

Kymri moved toward the doors, but Jori gripped her hand, searching her face.

"It's the only way to find her. Besides, Odson's got his friend helping us," she said softly. She hoped that actually meant something.

Expression set, he moved out ahead of her, then held out a hand to help her out. They both knew she didn't need the help despite the circumstances, she smiled at him.

They were led to a waiting plane on a small tarmac, where a crew member signaled the pilot to prepare as soon as they came into sight. The door was barely closed and they were rolling out to the runway. Kymri had never needed help flying before and she disliked it immensely. Jori seemed nonplussed by the situation.

She strained at her shackles to stretch her wings freely. Being at the mercy of someone else's flight habits was torture. Her dragon rumbled with discontent for the duration of the journey.

This was worse than the car.

We'll get out of this. We'll get out of this. We'll get out of this.

They had to find a way out. Or she'll have just handed Jori over to the dragon king that Elora had spent the last two decades protecting him from.

She studied his profile. He was looking out the small window, lost to his thoughts.

She wondered what they were. Surely, he was at least a little bit curious.

She'd never met her own sire. She didn't even know if he was dragon, human or other. Kolina never said a word about him. Kymri spent most of her life trying not to be curious but deep down it ate at her, fueling some of the resentment toward her mother.

She tried to imagine what Jori was feeling, not sure that she could, really. He grew up as a human chasing myths, only to find out they were real, and they were part of his heritage. He'd lost his mother only to discover she wasn't dead. Instead, she was living in captivity surrounded by the deadliest species on the planet. In order to keep him safe.

And here he was going into the dragon's den itself.

No, she couldn't imagine, not really.

She was scared, and she spent her life as a guardian for her people. Jori was an adventurer, not a warrior.

Until now. He would have to learn to be. Fast.

Otherwise, they might not survive.

T he plane's altitude shifted. They were preparing to land. Jori watched the ocean through his small window until the plane shifted again, bringing the landscape into view.

He recognized the mountain range cutting the sky from the ocean. He drew in a long deep breath, his heart racing. He'd been here before with his mother. They'd explored the lowlands, visiting villages in the valleys and along the coast.

He swallowed hard. Elora had taken a lot of risks to engage him with his heritage. Was every expedition a family history lesson?

He kept his eyes on the trajectory of the plane. He needed to know where they were going to land if they were going to figure out how to escape when they found her. How that was going to play out, he had no idea, but he couldn't leave her there. His father needed her. What would happen to him now that he was here? Would her captivity have been in vain? Had he just destroyed her attempts to save him? He couldn't bear to live with the knowledge that she was imprisoned for him. He would do what he had to.

The plane slid over the foothills toward the far side of the mountain and curled further inward. He looked for a runway, unable to see a strip breaking the trees far below them. The plane turned again, and he blinked.

He blinked again. Seriously? There was a fucking runway *in* the mountain? It was like a goddamned James Bond story. He may have considered himself an 'international man' but he sure as hell didn't have the skills of a spy heading into the Mastermind's lair. How the hell were they going to escape from a mountain lair? He glanced at Kymri.

They were so fucked.

He looked at the shackles on her wrists.

If he could figure out how to get those off of her, she had a shot at escape.

He glanced at their captors. How many of them were there?

The population of Kymri's island had hundreds of people inhabiting it. How many of them were dragons? If there was as much security here as there'd been on that island ... well, it sure as hell wasn't going to be a cakewalk. They'd figure something out.

Jori, there's a hell of a difference between a hungry jaguar and dragons with agendas.

Dragons.

This couldn't be fucking real.

The plane descended into the shadow of the mountains as they approached the cave mouth to land.

His stomach tilted and moments later the wheels touched down, bumping them to a halt.

Dragons with agendas.

Fan-fucking-tastic.

Chapter 19

Kymri's senses tracked every shift in altitude and direction, as they moved through the mountain corridors. It was as twisty as the queen's castle.

It would be difficult, but not impossible, to find their way out again. They would find a way.

She kept her eye on Jori as they walked. His tanned skin was pale, poor lighting aside. The severity of the situation was taking its toll on him. A human in a dragon lair, and his only potential allies were shackled and almost as vulnerable as he was.

The only thing to do now was meet their king and see what he had to say.

Jori had met Kymri's queen as though it were something he did all the time.

To be fair, he hadn't known about the dragons. Still, he had been a prisoner facing potential danger.

They turned a corner and she nearly gagged. The scent of male dragon assaulted her full force. She felt a flutter in her belly and shot Jori a glance. Male dragons were supposed to smell attractive to females, especially those in heat. But then, she was no longer in heat now, was she? Not only was she bonded, she was also carrying a youngling. Closing off any doors to other mates. Her gut rolled and she stumbled.

"Kymri?" Jori's concerned voice floated to her through a wave of nausea.

"I feel ill," she said, leaning against the wall as the scene before her twisted and wavered.

"What did you do to her? Did you poison her?" his voice was angry as he rounded on their captors.

"That's stupid, why they hell would we do that?" Clive snapped.

"How the fuck should I know?" Jori snapped back as he crouched down beside where she'd sunk to the floor.

"What's happening? How can I help?"

"It's the—the smell in here. It's overpowering," Kymri swallowed the excess saliva gathering in her mouth.

"What smell?"

"The stink of male dragon," she groaned.

"The stink of..." Jori sniffed the air, then lifted an arm, his expression blank.

She almost laughed, "Not you. Them."

"Get her to her feet," Stenlen commanded.

Clive and Merwin stepped forward, reaching for her. Their hands gripped her upper arms hard, forcing a hiss through her teeth.

"Sten, she is looking a little green."

"She was fine just minutes ago," he snapped.

"It's this place," she moaned, "too overpowering here."

"Sten if she hurls on me, so help her I'll bitch slap her into next Tuesday."

"No, Clive, you won't."

"Touch her and I'll kill you myself," Jori snarled.

Kymri was starting to smile at Jori while they were dragging her closer to the source of the stench. To her horror the gagging rose in severity, bringing up what little she had in her stomach along with it.

Just as they rounded the corner into a large open space she gagged, heaved and spilled her guts onto the floor, splattering Clive and Merwin's shoes.

She looked up to see dozens of faces staring with disgust in her direction.

She groaned and heaved again.

Her captors jumped aside to avoid any more mess on themselves.

Oh, dear dragon goddess, she couldn't believe this was happening to her.

J ori pulled his t-shirt off as Kymri wiped her mouth, "Here, cover your nose."

Her expression was grateful as she clamped the shirt over her face.

"Well, that was a dramatic introduction."

Jori's glare shot to the center of the crowded room, where a tall older man strode toward them, everyone falling away from his path. He moved with an easy grace—someone used to others moving out of his way. As on the island, this room was dominated by a singular sex. He stared back at the room of men looking on. Some were clearly disgusted, others bemused, most were curious.

Stenlen stepped forward to meet the approaching man. Clive and Merwin pulled Kymri forward. Jori remained as close to her as possible.

"Majesty," Stenlen said with a sharp bow. He frowned when Jori made no move to do likewise.

"Welcome, welcome." The man's smile was broad as he looked from Kymri to Jori. "Stenlen, find accommodations for our guests, would you?"

Guests?

He stopped before them; pure delight creased into a face that shockingly resembled his own. Seemingly oblivious to Kymri's state, he greeted her like a long-lost daughter, "Welcome, my dear." His voice softened as he turned his full attention on her.

She stiffened, glaring at him over the wad of t-shirt pressed to her face.

"I'm delighted to welcome a female into our home. You need not worry; you will be given every comfort." He then turned to Jori, eyes glittering in the low light. "Is this him, Stenlen?"

"It is, sire."

"Ah, my boy," his voice had gone very soft as he moved closer to Jori, looking him over like a proud new father.

He almost expected him to count his fingers and toes.

Jori's glance swept the room again. Every pair of eyes were trained on him as he stared into his biological father's face. The same jaw line, familiar slope to the nose and set of the brow. There was no doubt they were related.

"Where is my mother?"

Pride glittered in the older man's eyes. His smile widened as he assessed Jori as though from a new angle.

Jori remained as he was.

"You'll meet her at the initiation. I can see that you have been sorely neglected in our ways. That shall be remedied at our earliest convenience."

"I want to see her now."

Stenlen growled. The older man held up his hand and he ceased immediately. "You are tired after your long journey, I'm sure a good rest will remind you of your manners in polite society. We will chat again soon." With a nod to Stenlen, he turned away. Kymri was being dragged back down the hall. Jori stared after the king as he strode back to the end of the room. No one else had moved.

He turned and followed Kymri to ensure they didn't hurt her no matter what Stenlen said. He wouldn't leave her side.

They were led back through the maze of artificially lit identical halls, emerging into an area that was clearly different from the rest of the place. Where the complex had been stark and utilitarian, this area appeared to be more residential. It lacked the grandeur of the castle island. In opposition, this place was fully modern, with gleaming floors and stark lines and angles in the materials and fixtures. The only decorative relief he could see were signets breaking the austerity.

Their steps echoed over the hard floor as they turned yet another corner. Adorning the wall at the end of the hall was a large, singular, signet shield.

In the island citadel, there had been many signet banners adorning the Assembly hall. So far as he could tell, there was only one here. It was familiar too. It appeared in some of his mother's art that was dark and heavy. Art that he never copied to adorn his body as tattoos like her other pieces.

He observed their route as much as possible, in order to try to find their way out again— once they found his mother. The king wouldn't let him see her until they initiated him.

He swallowed. Kymri's attitude about this wasn't encouraging; she acted as though he'd lose his sense of self.

That would never happen.

His mind drifted back to what Odson had told him about his mother's experiences with this man. She'd been terrified of him and she'd been locked away here for —how long? More than a decade.

He had no illusions of what might have been done to her, and he prayed he was wrong. Human or not, he'd die to get her and Kymri out of here if he had to.

He'd do whatever it took to gain their freedom.

Chapter 20

I t was all she could do to fight the overwhelming stench of male dragon. Thankfully, Jori's shirt pressed to her nose help soothe her nerves so she could control her stomach.

This had to be a side effect of the pregnancy.

Dragons didn't get sick. Not like this.

She wondered if the problem was exacerbated by the bond with Jori. The bond and the pregnancy made all other males smell terrible to her senses. It was such a difference from how she'd reacted to Jori's scent when she'd gone into heat. She couldn't get enough of him, and now, it was providing comfort.

Distracted as she was, she'd barely been able to focus on what the older man was saying to them before she was being dragged away again down unending halls.

Finally, they stopped in front of a door identical to every other door in the place. It was whipped open and she was shoved inside, then the door slammed shut before she could utter a word to Jori, who'd instantly tried to stop it from separating them. She could hear him yelling through the barrier. There was no handle this side of the door, so she pounded on it with her fist, "Jori!"

Through the door, his curses echoed in the stark hall. There were grunts and thuds and another door slammed.

Pressing her ear to the door, she could still hear his curses, though now muffled, and a faint thudding.

Closing her eyes, she sighed, resting her forehead to the wood for a long moment before turning to inspect the room she'd been thrown into.

Bed, chairs, bathroom. Simple.

They were deep in the mountain; the door would be the only way in and out of the room. Still, she looked about the room for a creative escape. No hidden access panels, the air duct was long and narrow. There was a tiny camera in the corner of the ceiling.

She sighed, bringing her hand up to brush the hair from her face, her new bracelet caught her eye.

If she could get these bloody things off, she could at least shift. She'd told Jori the king was the only individual that could remove them. As far as she knew. That didn't stop her from trying to tug her hands free. They appeared seamless.

Flipping the chair over, she inspected it for any loose parts. If she worked on some way to break the cuffs, maybe she could also figure out how to get Jori and Elora out of the mountain alive.

Jori's pacing was interrupted by the opening of his prison door. The king sauntered in with a smile. Stenlen and his cronies blocked the exit behind him.

"I thought you could use this, since you gave yours to your female."

Jori looked at the offered shirt in the king's hand.

He accepted it with a nod and pulled it on. The expensive fabric didn't go with his shorts and hiking boots, but what the hell.

"Shall we begin again?"

A young man brought in a tray of food and set it on the end of the bed, formally acknowledged the king and backed out of the room.

Jori didn't demand to see his mother again, or Kymri, instead he waited to see what it was that this man wanted from him. The king assessed him.

"You do look like your mother—an attractive female, without a doubt. I am pleased how strongly you resemble myself and my fore-bears. This is good." He paused a moment, "You may call me Rich-mund. Jori... Mountainside, is it?"

He nodded.

"It is a good name. Good of your foster father to name you as his. But you will use your proper name from now on. Kargassa." He clamped a hand on Jori's should and gave it a pat of what he thought passed for affection.

Like fuck. "I won't change my name."

"Hm. You'll get used to it," he waved a hand and went on, "your female is carrying your child, yes?"

He didn't answer.

"So quiet," he mused, "takes after his mother," he said to Stenlen with a laugh.

Stenlen stood in the doorway glaring at Jori.

Clearly, he didn't like what he perceived to be Jori's impertinence toward their leader.

"What do you want from me?"

Stenlen tensed.

The king turned his shrewd gaze on Jori. "Far more like your mother than I care for." The king's face hardened, his eyes became icy, his smile brittle. "Just to have my son at my side. What more could there be?"

"I have no interest in staying here."

Stenlen growled.

"Close the door, I wish a moment with my progeny." his hand flicked him away.

"Sire—"

The king stared at Stenlen, who in turn closed the door without another protest.

Jori had watched his mother negotiate with many stubborn merchants during their travels. While he lacked his mother's diplomatic skills, he at least strove for her patience in difficult situations.

"What do you want from life, Jori?"

Here it was. He shrugged. "Never really thought too hard on the subject," he lied.

He thought about it all the time. All the things he wanted in life really came down to independence and family. He wanted the autonomy to roam the world as he pleased and the comfort and love of a family he could share his life with.

The king's eyes narrowed on Jori's face. He sighed. "I've seen some of your videos. You probably don't realize how much you tell of yourself in them. Your love of adventure and your desire to reconnect with your mother. Very touching." He smiled. "Let me tell you a secret. Living among dragons can be incredibly adventurous. You could work with Stenlen to scout and find other dragon hives. We are a brotherhood. You wouldn't have to be alone anymore. And your mother is here whenever you wish to see her." He reached toward the bowl of strawberries on the tray and popped one into his mouth. "These are good, you should have some."

Jori ignored the offered fruit. "You went to a lot of trouble to bring us here. What do you *think* I can do for you in this mountain kingdom of yours?"

The king sighed again, "It was a lot of trouble, wasn't it? Your mother kept me from you. I have rights as a father."

"To what end?" Jori ground his teeth.

"As I said, a father has rights to his child. By the way, I'm very, very pleased there is a grandchild on the way. Very pleased." He smiled.

Jori's stomach flipped.

"Really though," Richmund continued, chewing the last strawberry from the bunch he'd taken from the tray, "eat your food, the initiation will begin soon. Your mother will be there, you can catch up with her at the reception afterward. She'll be stunned to see you, I know." He rapped on the door, then turned back as it opened. "Oh, and don't get too used to this room; after the initiation, you'll be moved to more appropriate accommodations. Much nicer." He smiled again. "Big screen tv and great sound system."

The door closed behind him.

The king wanted his offspring. He wanted Jori's child too. A dynasty. He wanted to establish a dynasty. But through all of that, he guessed his real goal was still the queen herself. Otherwise why bother with the island? His mother had been a convenient alternative. Back up insurance.

Offspring were vital to continue the lineage. Now they had two fertile women in captivity. His mother—Jori caught his breath. Had she been forced to bear more children? He hated that she undoubtedly had been forced into sex with that delusional bastard. A little ripple went through his gut at the thought of siblings, though he hadn't seen any young faces in the hall. That didn't mean anything, they might have just been elsewhere.

If there were younger children, why would he push so hard to have Jori brought here? He'd have others to fill whatever role it was that he thought Jori could do.

It didn't matter. He needed to figure out what he could do to obtain his mother's and Kymri's freedom. As much as he hated the idea of being trapped in a mountain, he couldn't stand the thought of them being forced to live here under the yoke of forced childbearing.

Chapter 21

——————

Kymri's wrists were raw from the constant tugging on the shackles binding her dragon magic. If it weren't for her ability to heal quickly, the flesh would be scraped to the bone. The metal was just too snug. Dislocating her thumb did nothing but cause a lot of pain. Thankfully, she was able to get it back in place properly. It had given her something to concentrate on and get her overloaded senses under control.

Footsteps echoed in the corridor outside her door seconds before it swung open. A young male glanced at the tray of barely eaten food then held clothing aloft. "The king wishes you to dress appropriately for his progeny's initiation. We may leave as soon as you have changed."

"If I don't?"

"Then you may not attend. He would prefer it if you did."

She snatched it from his hand.

Expression impassive, he closed the door.

Stripping off her shirt and jeans, she tossed them on the bed and pulled the dress over her head. She wondered who it I was made for, if anyone in particular. It didn't quite fit properly. The neckline plunged despite being too snug to look right, and the hem dragged on the floor. Pulling her boots back on under the dress relieved some of the drag.

Before knocking on the door, she grabbed Jori's t-shirt from where she'd left it neatly folded. She might need it. She prayed she'd be able to control herself this time—vomiting was disgusting.

Clutching the shirt in her hands, she stepped out to follow the young male and several more fell in line as escort. Her stomach rolled at the cloud of male dragon scents. Concentrating on steadying her breathing, she followed, seriously hoping the inconvenient illness would pass.

Kymri was not taken to the same hall they'd been to on their arrival. She was led deeper down into the mountain, arriving at a set of massive wooden doors resembling those at the citadel. Older, more primitive.

The air here was different, colder, and earthier. There was lighting, but the central air system didn't extend this far down.

Goosebumps skittered over her arms. Her dragon was paying close attention. She was about to enter an ancient space, apart from the living world. This was a space of magic and ritual. Power.

Her queen protected a similar space.

Stepping through the doors, she was led along a torch-lit natural rock corridor, some hewn, the rest mostly natural cave formation.

Her dragon stretched within her, basking in the vibration of the earth feeding her magic, seeking the particular tenor of the minerals. She could visually pick out the striations of the ore. Breathing deeply, as they moved along, she gave her dragon space to absorb the vibrational energy of the ore that glittered in the firelight.

She was surrounded by her element. Her flesh crackled as the power worked its way in toward her bones. The will of her magic pushed at the will of the king's magic infused into her shackles, but it wasn't enough.

Another set of doors swung open on silent hinges and she stared into the vastness of the cave at the heart of the mountain. The power was tangible, exhilarating. Her eyes swept the space, taking in the numbers of males attending the event, and the massive dragon dominating view.

Dangerous bone spur spikes jutted from the top of his head and in jagged rows down his back. His eyes were like pools of lava, his scales resembling rippling layers of dried blood.

The king was in dragon form and he was larger than any dragon she'd seen before. Among her own kind, her queen's dragon was larger than her subjects, as was expected. She swallowed the fear that thrummed through her. This colony was equal to her island's population, but they were all larger. During the attack, it had taken two or three guardians to fend off each of the three invaders.

This is what her people were now exposed and vulnerable to. She had to find a way to protect her queen and her people. It was what she lived for. She had to find a way.

Kymri's escort led her right up toward the front of the cave, to the edge of the cleared space where the ceremony was going to happen.

Jori wasn't here yet, nor was Elora.

Her dragon pushed out, searching for him through their bond, filigree threads reaching for his hidden dragon.

He was near.

Despite his discomfort at moving deeper into the maw of the earth, Jori could not deny the presence of power. It was the power all ancient civilizations spoke of. A place that invited temples and shrines to be erected. A place where gods were created and worshiped. And buried and forgotten.

Stenlen had come for him. Ordered him to strip and don a robe.

He felt ridiculous. Like he was being led to sacrifice for some freaky cult ritual.

This was his chance to make contact with his mother. They wouldn't allow him to see her until the ritual was complete. Whatever they would do to him, so be it. He'd figure out how to get her and Kymri away from these nutcases afterward.

The massive wooden doors opened. His heart stopped and restarted at a frantic pace, forcing him to struggle against his own instinct to run from danger.

All he could see was the dragon dominating everything, its glittering eyes trained on him. It looked as though it might be smiling, but he couldn't be sure of the thin reptilian lips stretched over huge pointed teeth, lining a jaw that could crush him whole.

Holy fuck.

Jori curled his hands into fists to hide their tremor and forced deep steady breaths into his lungs.

Something drew his attention away from the predator. A little brush of consciousness. Tentative and gentle. His eyes found Kymri turned toward him, her expression unreadable. The sensation that floated between them increased and his heart rate slowed so that the rushing in his ears eased.

I love you.

His attention turned back toward his biological father, looming before him. Jori walked, alone, out into the open space before the dragon king.

Planting his bare feet on the ice-cold stone floor he didn't flinch when Stenlen removed the robe from his shoulders, leaving him naked before everyone gathered. He focused on the beast before him, aware of the tether of Kymri's presence, pushing the extreme sense of vulnerability to the back of his mind. He straightened his spine and set his shoulders.

The only sound in the room was that of the dragon's slow, steady breathing.

Was there actually some kind of a ritual, or was Jori about to be consumed by this thing?

For all the sticky situations he'd been in over the years, he'd finally met one he didn't think he'd be able to wriggle out of, scathed or not.

The dragon drew in a long deep breath, pulling at Jori.

His gaze remained forward, his body taut. His thoughts turned again to Kymri, somewhere behind him, standing as witness.

A claw loomed into view, stretching toward him, then swiped across his chest. He jerked against the sudden pain searing his flesh, but he swallowed down the urge to cry out.

The claw sliced the flesh of the dragon's snout. As the blood welled, Richmund pushed his bleeding snout against Jori's bleeding chest.

The dragon's eyes closed.

The air rippled around him - like it had rippled around Kymri when she shifted into her dragon form before him.

He could still feel Kymri's presence brushing at the back of his neck.

The ripple grew more intense and he could feel the pull toward the dragon. He resisted the urge to learn forward toward it.

Then came a peculiar sensation creeping outward from the fresh wound. It oozed through him, seeking vessels to travel along. The ripple became a buffer around him, slowly blocking out everything but the sensation of the dragon's essence infusing him.

He didn't like it.

A deep, guttural growl rose up his throat.

His pulse increased and his mind tried to will the sensation to stop its spread, invading his body. As he did so, the will of the dragon intensified to dominate him, wearing at his resistance.

There was a sudden pop in his mind, and he felt as though he stood on a narrow precipice staring at an abyss. The sense of vertigo was overwhelming as he struggled to catch his breath.

Whispers invaded his thoughts.

Accept me.

Accept my will.

Serve my will.

I am your Liege.

No.

The words repeated. Jori denied them again, his subconscious grasping the fragile thread connecting him to Kymri. The words came again, and again, each time louder and with more force. The thread began to fray, floating across the void. The dragon's words were the solid ledge on which he stood.

He denied them.

Until he couldn't.

Chapter 22

Kymri's dragon fed her the power they'd absorbed from the raw ore of the mountain walls. She funneled it all into the bond thread she cast to Jori. She knew he could sense her. She could feel his response to her presence and echoed her sentiment.

I love you.

It reverberated back and forth along the length of their psychic thread.

Through it, she could feel the emotional turmoil he was experiencing as the dragon king recited the ritual to bend him to his will, to force his loyalty.

The ritual was meant to be voluntary.

She could feel Jori's resistance, and she had no idea what that would do to him as the dragon pressed harder on his mind.

Visually, little was happening.

Jori stood naked, his body strung so taut he looked as though he could snap. Every muscle was flexed and rigid with the strain of the power being forced on his human form—his subservient form.

Her throat was tight, her heart hammered in her chest.

She was dimly aware of the doors opening behind them as air whispered around the massive cavern.

She dared not look, as she desperately held onto Jori.

A tall woman drifted into her line of sight, her gaze glued on the scene before all of them, her expression impassive.

Assessing.

She frowned. Confusion crept across her features, her lips thinned, brows furrowed.

Her lips parted with a gasp, and the concentrated frown sprang loose as her expression twisted back and forth between joy and pain.

Elora.

A thin band of metal hugged her slim throat.

Her eyes slid between Jori and the dragon, and rage descended over her as she drew breath. A ripple of power surged around them as Elora screamed words so ancient, Kymri had no idea what they meant, but her dragon reacted with shock, making her lose concentration on her thread.

Everyone seemed to be affected by the trigger of recognition, hearing words only their deepest dragon understood. It shocked the king, causing enough distraction to pull his attention from Jori.

The effect on Jori was instant.

Released from the onslaught, his body sagged.

Terror ripped through Kymri. What had Elora done? Had she killed him?

Jori didn't fall to the floor, he caught himself on a knee, the air shimmering around him. It intensified.

A deafening roar emanated from a throat incapable of making such a sound.

It resonated through her, snatching an involuntary gasp of awe and desire. Her dragon was fully alert, straining against the magic of the shackles repressing her as Jori's dragon emerged.

Oh.

He was magnificent!

The torchlight made the deep green of his scales shimmer. His claws were razor hooks. His opalescent eyes were otherworldly.

The crowd flowed away as he filled the space.

The dragon king stumbled into the cave wall.

J ori struggled to regain his breath, exhilarated and terrified by what was happening.

Kymri's whisper in his head—*I love you*—had been replaced by the forced dominance of Richmund's monstrous voice luring him into submission.

Then, he could have sworn he'd heard his mother; a rage-filled shout that struck his heart, and everything changed.

Released, the air around him changed and he was melting. Everything that he was, disintegrated, warped to make room for something else, adding to himself. Growing.

Was he having an out of body experience? Richmund had killed him, and this was Jori leaving his carcass behind as he floated upward like a helium balloon to the cave roof. When he looked down, he didn't actually feel weightless. He was very solid, but so very high up.

He looked down on his father, the dragon king.

That pathetic little dragon had tried to suppress his will and make him subservient. How dare he? He deserved to be crushed.

Anger shot through his body, white hot. He felt a pull on his lower back, turning in time to see a heavy tail whipping through the space. His own tail lashed back and forth, expressing his agitation.

Then he noticed the little people staring up at him in awe.

Kymri stared up at him in awe.

His female.

But she was too small. She was human.

He wanted to see her dragon.

He bent his head toward her, sniffing.

The scent of Richmund's magic shackled her. Confined her.

His large head swung back to the dragon king and he growled in his face.

You are not my king. I have no king. I answer to no one.

The king lunged at him, teeth snapping. *You will submit.*

All of Jori's life had been lived in peaceful existence. Loving his parents, adventures around the world, taking life in stride. He had never felt the need to control events around him, never struck out at another. Acts of violence were acts of survival.

What thrummed through him now was pure and raw. The instinct to destroy what had tried to dominate him blurred his vision and filled his chest. His fist-claws curled with the desire to strike and rip. To claim and make this place, these servants, his own. These females his own. He was power and they were there to serve him.

Jori's human brain was screaming inside him, but his dragon did not wish to hear such a feeble voice.

The dragon king lunged again.

Yet Jori could smell Richmund's fear as he went on the offensive.

The king would make Jori submit to his will or he would kill him.

All or nothing.

Chapter 23

Kymri stumbled backward along with everyone else to allow for the extra space needed to accommodate Jori's size. The cave, as large as it was, had suddenly become claustrophobic.

The king's guards were shouting to move in, but there wasn't enough room for them to shift. Some were scrambling to figure out how to help their king. Everyone else looked on as though it were a spectator sport. Spotting Elora on the far side, her back to the cave wall, Kymri, pushed her way toward her.

"Kymri Steelscale?" The shock of seeing her son was still etched into her features as she turned to Kymri in recognition.

"Madam Ambassador, how do we remove these shackles?"

Elora blinked, "I uhm, the king, he has to touch them and release the spell."

"How do we get out of here?"

"With great difficulty, if you can't fly."

Kymri bristled at the sound of Stenlen's voice shouting over the sound of snarling dragons echoing through the cave.

She turned, snarling at him, putting herself between Elora and the male.

"You won't be going anywhere until the king decides you may."

Clive and Merwin moved in, surrounding the women.

"I suggest we move out of the way while our king puts his son in his place."

"I'm not leaving without him," Elora spat. "How the hell did he get here?"

"It's a long story."

The ground shook as the king stomped the cave floor with a roar, lunging for Jori's throat. Jori roared back, swiping his claws across the king's face, leaving behind sliced flesh. Blood flew through the air, speckling everything within range.

Jori wasn't submitting.

This was unprecedented. Dragons accepted their liege.

Kymri recalled he'd laughingly mentioned he had problems with authority.

She turned to Elora, who watched the skirmish with a mix of awe and fear. "I did everything I could to avoid this."

They scrambled out of the way as Jori's tail whipped past them, slamming into the wall over their heads. Several rocks tumbled free.

The group's movement caught the attention of the king, who slammed his own tail down as a barrier, trapping both the women and their guards. Ducking another swipe of Jori's claws, he reached out his own and grabbed Elora.

Crushed in his grip, the king pulled her up in front of Jori's face.

"Jori, don't submit to him," Elora screamed. "Don't!"

Kymri realized she meant to die to stop it from happening if she had to.

Of course she would, she'd spent Jori's lifetime trying to stop all of this from happening, she wasn't about to let the years go to waste.

Jori went still. Growling filled the room.

The tip of the king's claw moved to the center of Elora's chest.

Kymri heard Stenlen suck his breath in.

"Kill the bitch, my liege!" Clive shouted, as he pinned a knife to Kymri's throat.

"Drop the knife, Clive," Stenlen ordered.

"Fuck you, Sten. If that little prick doesn't submit to the king, we'll make him."

"The females are not to be harmed. Ever."

"Clearly the king doesn't agree with you."

The king's claw was pressed to Elora's chest, whose head was thrown back in pain. Even though she wasn't human, she couldn't withstand the strength of the dragon. With that throat shackle, she was vulnerable and fragile.

Kymri's dragon screamed out from deep within her, causing her to struggle blindly against her captor, ignoring the sharp blade scraping the delicate flesh of her throat. Everything in her was determined to protect Elora.

Jori backed away from the king.

The king moved toward his men, roughly released Elora to the floor and began shifting back to human form.

He looked up into Jori's dragon face, "I will destroy them if you do not submit," Richmund said.

Elora rolled to her knees, struggling to her feet.

Kymri glanced at Stenlen to her left. The conflict was plain on his face. "Don't think your bastard of a king won't do it," she hissed.

"Shut up!" Clive barked, jerking her head back by the hair.

"There's a reason we've been hidden all this time," she rasped.

"Jori," Elora pulled his attention, "he'll use you to destroy the queen's sanctuary. He—"

The king backhanded her so hard that she careened into the rough cave wall and crumpled in a daze. Following, he grabbed her limp form, hauling her upright, his fist clamped hard around her throat above the thin band of metal.

Kymri felt the truth of her words strike her heart. "Jori, I won't allow it! I'll do everything in my power to protect that sanctuary—you know it!" She was as willing to destroy herself as Elora had been.

"You're both tedious. I made the mistake of letting this one live among us." Richmund waved toward Elora's limp form. "You, I think I'll keep out of sight until I wish to use you."

"I'd like to see you fucking try." she challenged him.

He approached her, a grin splitting his face, "I grow weary of niceties and ritual. It's time to just get on with things." His hand grabbed her crotch. "When I've had my fill of you, maybe I'll let my loyal men have theirs, then we'll go find this island and take what is rightfully ours."

Merwin laughed, "I look forward to it."

"I'll kill you if you try," Kymri snarled.

"This is going to be fun. Go on, struggle," he gripped her harder, "that's more fun."

Kymri was jostled and Clive's knife nicked her throat as Stenlen slammed into him. Suddenly free of restraint, Kymri knocked into the king, throwing her forehead into his face before stumbling toward Elora's prone form.

Stenlen struggled against Clive and Merwin to gain control of the knife.

The king staggered from the impact, clutching his face as blood streamed from his nostrils.

Jori roared, his jaws coming down over the king, shaking him like a rag doll and whipping him across the length of the cavern to slam against the wall. As soon as he hit the floor, Jori's paw came down, his claw impaling the king's chest.

The shackles fell away.

Kymri and Elora were free.

Clive and Merwin froze.

The king was dead.

All of those gathered that had remained in the recesses to watch the proceedings stood silent, staring at the king's body. Most were expressionless. Some looked satisfied. They all looked to Jori, who unwaveringly stared back at them. They eventually began sinking to a knee before him.

Long live the king.

Jori's large head swung toward Clive and Merwin, snarling. Terror filled their faces.

"I think he is displeased with you," Stenlen said dryly.

Kymri's hand touched his snout, drawing his attention. She was pale and smelled of the blood that slid from her wound.

The haze of rage subsided. He blinked at her.

"Release the magic, Jori."

He wasn't sure how. But he concentrated on her face and being able to speak to her. Slowly, the room shimmered and he descended to her level.

He struggled to stop the trembling that wracked his body as Kymri slid into his embrace.

"The first time shocks the body, it doesn't know what to do with the power."

He gripped her hard against him, breathing in the scent of her hair.

He had just killed a man. He had killed his biological father.

He opened his eyes, seeking out his mother.

She stood just behind Kymri, her eyes drinking him in.

Was she really there?

He drew in a deep breath and let it out with a shudder.

Someone brought Jori's robe. Kymri quickly helped him slip into it before he turned to his mother.

She looked rough.

Her hand rested on her throat, her eyes large pools in the dim torchlight.

"Mom."

She broke into a watery smile and he shot forward to hug her.

She was so much smaller than he remembered, but then, he'd grown into a man since the last time he'd been able to hug his mother.

His throat was too thick for words. Her body shuddered as she cried quietly, whispering, "My boy."

He didn't know how long they stood like that before she eventually pulled away, sniffling and wiping the tears from her face, smiling at him.

"You've grown so much."

"You haven't." He grinned, gaining a laugh from her.

He glanced around for Kymri. The entire cavern had been cleared out, and the king's body removed. She stood sentinel by the enormous doors.

"I'm sorry for all of this. I tried to keep it away from you for as long as possible."

"It was a lot to take in when reality started to hit. I never actually dreamed dragons were real, let alone that I was one of them."

Elora's face flushed with shame, "I hope you understand, I had to bind your dragon magic to keep you hidden from him. It was the only way."

"Ma, it's okay. Really." He studied her a moment, "So, am I going to turn into a dragon every time you shout whatever it was you said?"

She smiled, "No, that was just the unbinding spell. It's all up to you now."

"I see," he said with a sigh.

"We have a lot of catching up to do," Elora said.

"We do." he squeezed her hand, "Dad will be beside himself when he sees you."

His mother's face dropped, her lip trembled, "I don't think that's a good idea."

"Why not?"

"Because I left him; he must be so angry with me."

"No, Ma. He loves you. He needs you."

"Maybe," she hedged, turning her attention to Kymri. "I see you made it home."

He turned, letting his eyes roam over his mate as they moved toward the doors, "I sure did."

Chapter 24

Kymri stood next to Jori, holding his hand in hers. His thumb stroked her fingers. He seemed unable to not be touching her at any given moment.

They were in Elora's room.

"What happens now?" he asked his mother, "I can't believe they all just walked away like that when I killed their king. Shouldn't they have ripped me apart?"

"They had no right to step in. As his heir, you're the only one that had the right to challenge him for dominance."

"I don't understand it all. If it was a possibility that I could do that, why risk bringing me here in the first place."

"He was incredibly arrogant. As far as he was concerned, he was all powerful, and you would submit to his will. As his heir, it shows he has progeny to support his legacy and a weapon in his arsenal against the queen." Elora studied her son for a long moment. "It never would have occurred to him that you wouldn't submit. That was never part of his world."

"So, everyone else is just going to do my bidding now?" he asked, skeptical.

"Doubtful," Kymri said. "You'll still have to prove yourself to be a strong leader. Clearly, you're strong enough to take the throne, but that doesn't mean anything in terms of leadership."

Jori snorted, "I want to be a king less than I wanted to submit to one."

Elora's expression was grim, "If you don't, they will continue to be a threat to the queen.

Kymri thought of Clive and Merwin. "Some of those guys believe they have the right to dominate the female dragons. It's been their mission all their lives. That's not simply going to go away. There's an entire tribe of male dragons indoctrinated with that belief. The king deliberately cultivated that."

Jori scrubbed a hand over his face, "I don't want anything to do with this. I just wanted to bring you home to Dad. Fuck them. Fuck all of them."

"And my people? Fuck them too?" Kymri spat, pulling away from him.

Jori's gaze shot to her face, "No, of course not.

"Jori, if they are left to scatter, they will attack the sanctuary."

"Unless someone changes things from within, the threat will never go away." Kymri's hand slid to her belly.

His gaze fell to the movement of her hand, changing his expression. They had a child.

A male child would have to be guided.

A female child would live under threat.

She thought about how all of this might change everything.

According to her own people, she would be expected to live on the island with her female child. If she bore a son, he would not be permitted to live among them.

Nor would Jori, in either case.

He didn't want to be king.

She didn't want to leave her people.

But she didn't want to leave him either.

There was so much to consider.

She looked at Elora. Her hand rubbed at the discolored line across her throat where the band had been.

She must be one hell of a diplomat to have survived all this time here. Or she must be one hell of a survivor.

She was sure Elora hadn't been treated as an honored guest and paid the respect an ambassador deserved. She had no illusions as to what she might have endured to be here.

Elora wasn't broken.

Despite being guardian commander, Kymri doubted she'd be able to say the same, had she been the one to suffer through Elora's ordeals. Her hand slid across her womb again, her gaze returning to Jori.

She supposed it depended on what held you together.

What the fuck was he supposed to do now?

He had no fucking idea how to be a dragon king. He didn't know any of these guys.

He could walk away, go back to his life traveling the world.

Alone.

Alone, because he sure as hell knew Kymri wouldn't leave her people unprotected.

She also said they couldn't be together on her island anyway.

In what scenario would they ever have had a shot?

He glanced at his mother. She'd been forced into leaving in order to protect him. If he hadn't been under threat, would she have gone back and let him be raised by his father?

Maybe.

Things change.

Lives change.

No one ever goes back.

"What will you do now?"

Elora's expression turned grim, brow creased, then cleared. "That depends on you."

"And you?" he asked Kymri.

"I have to say my answer also depends on you."

The expectation on their faces was crushing. His muscles began to itch, forcing him to move. He needed to get out of this place. This suffocating mountain. He felt the need to expand. He hated confined places. He needed to see the sky, the stars.

"I need some air," he said, leaving them in the room.

Stalking the halls, he tried to remember the rough direction they'd come from, until he ran into someone. The next person he saw happened to be the guy who had brought meals to him during his imprisonment.

"I want to go outside, where's the way out?"

He gave a short bow, "This way, sire."

Jori sighed.

The man stole a curious glance as they walked.

"What is it?"

"Master Stenlen may be a good ally for you, sire. He has always been loyal to the throne."

Jori snorted, "And his goons?"

"Goons, sire."

They turned a corner and faced a set of steel doors. The man pressed his thumb to the keypad, which scanned the digit.

This wasn't the way they'd come in.

They stepped into the elevator. There were a surprising amount of buttons for floors to access.

"What's your name?"

"Eamerson, sire."

"Jori Mountainside." He held out his hand.

He hesitated but shook it.

The doors opened. They stepped into an ultra-modern room, all hard angles and gleaming surfaces. It was vast, feeling more so with the floor to ceiling windows lining the entirety of the far side.

It reminded him of the assembly room he'd been taken to, to stand trial before the queen. Its size was comparable, and it too had been surrounded by massive arched windows.

"Is this where the council meets?"

"Council, sire?"

"Council—you know, where people meet to make decisions?"

"There is no council. This is the king's room to use for whatever he wished." He moved toward the windows. His hand brushed the glass and a huge pane slid open. Fresh mountain air rushed in, and drew Jori out toward the open space. They were nestled into the side of the mountain overlooking a rolling valley carpeted with thick pines.

No council. A king in his high castle overlooking the world, his people beneath him in the bowels of the mountain.

The queen had her citadel overlooking her island. A queen that had ejected the entire male population. This felt different.

Where else could they have gone? Of course they would try to find their own kind. After centuries of forced enmity, it was no wonder their worlds had come to this.

The king preyed on the young men, trapping them in an endless cycle to feed his power.

He hadn't meant to kill the king. He had just wanted to free his mother and Kymri from enslavement.

Kymri.

She had spent her life protecting her people from that very enslavement which he'd tried to save her from. She would have done anything to protect them. Anything.

He recalled the day she pulled a knife on him to secure the batteries of his equipment. She'd been prepared to kill him.

He had no doubt she had been prepared to do so again, had he submitted to the will of the king.

Luckily for him, things went a little differently.

Jori stepped out onto the large platform. Large enough for a dragon.

His chest rumbled.

Eamerson stepped back into the room with a short bow.

Jori stripped, dropping his clothes in a pile beside the open glass. Moving to the center of the platform he breathed deeply and closed his eyes searching.

Come on then.

His body tingled, his breath puffed and heart raced.

Opening his eyes, his vantage point was dizzyingly higher as he looked down at himself, nearly filling the enormous platform.

His chest rumbled again.

Finally free.

He flexed his wings.

He thought of the little plane he'd flown with his mother—the one that had brought him to Kymri.

Wanting nothing more than to launch off the edge, he held back.

His dragon protested.

He felt as though.... As though if he gave into this one thing—this most natural thing, to fly as a dragon—there would be no going back. Not ever.

He stepped to the edge, his powerful claws gripping the thick stone.

He drew a great breath, flexed his wings again, moving them a little to get a sense of how they worked attached to his back, and stared out over the expanse.

With another breath, he hoped like fuck that he wouldn't drop like a stone headfirst into the ground and launched himself, wings snapping out hard.

His heart pounded as the ground rushed by and there was nothing but icy air filling his lungs and enveloping his wings and body.

Pure exhilaration.

Nothing he'd done before could compare to this.

Not the jungle treks, the desert caravans, or the mountain climbing.

He just hoped he could figure out how to land without killing himself.

His dragon chuckled.

You always do.

Yeah, true.

Chapter 25

Kymri followed the quiet man who led her and Elora through the corridors and up an elevator.

They stepped out into a massive room with a breathtaking view.

Jori was a shadow to the side, facing out. He turned as their footsteps echoed closer.

Elora walked several steps behind Kymri as they approached, and stopped several paces away.

Turning in their direction, she could see the light in his eyes.

Something had changed since they'd seen him downstairs. The haggard shock was clearing, making room for something new.

Her breath caught as he looked at her. Her dragon purred.

She spared a glance at Elora, whose expression was strained. Noticing Kymri's regard, she smiled, forcing her face to relax.

"Memories," she murmured, "the king's personal room. His every whim was concocted here, and sometimes executed." Elora smiled up at Jori, waiting for what he wanted to say.

"The queen had a grand assembly room at her citadel," he said, turning toward the empty space. "What do you think?"

"Nicer view than the one in the basement," Kymri said.

Elora's eyes crinkled, "I think it's a good start, Jori." Her shoulders sagged in relief.

"There's a phone in the other room, I made a couple of calls while waiting for you." He reached out to touch Elora's shoulder. "Odson's friends were able to grab satellite Intel to track where we are, and they're already on their way here. Dad is with him."

Elora blanched, straightening her shoulders like any experienced diplomat facing uncertain negotiations.

"I don't know what I'm doing here, Ma. I need all the help I can get."

She nodded. "I'll just, uhm, go and prepare myself," she said, turning to go.

Before she went, Jori caught her shoulder again and wrapped his arms around her. "I love you, Ma."

She wrapped her arms around him tightly, sagging into his arms, "I've missed you so hard." She breathed, sniffling.

"He'll be here soon." Jori cleared her tears with his thumbs and leaned down to kiss her forehead.

Once she reached the door, Jori reached for Kymri's hand.

"This bond you said we have?"

She looked up into his face, uncertainty stilled his features.

"What does it mean?"

"It means, we have a bond that will last the rest of our lives. We are only for each other."

"Is there ever a choice?"

Her heart stopped. She stepped away from him. "There is always a choice. But we will always be connected."

Was he going to step into the king's shoes and proposition the queen? She hadn't thought him ambitious, but then, his world had completely changed in a very short time.

She looked at him, trying to read his thoughts. Was Jori about to ask her to step into the role of consort with their child in her belly?

"I've been on my own for most of my life," he said. "Don't like being told what to do, or how to live. Never wanted to be tied down to any one place or person. I wanted the freedom to fly at will."

"I-I see," she whispered. So this was it. It was for the best. The queen would never have allowed him to live on the island. He was too much of a threat. She supposed, even more so now.

"I've lived my entire life to protect my queen and my people," she said.

"And things change."

"That won't. Not ever."

He nodded. "Maybe we can help each other."

Her brow shot up, "How so?"

"It seems I've got a mountain full of disillusioned dragons that need to be educated—me included—on proper dragon relations."

"You think I can be a teacher?"

Jori shrugged, "I thought maybe Mom would help teach them, and you could help keep them in line."

"A warden."

"Something like that. Whatever you want, if you will stay with me."

Her chest froze.

Stay?

"If I have to be king, then I'll need a queen and an heir. I think you fit the profile. If you want it."

Queen?

Could she? What of her fealty to her own queen?

"I don't know, Jori."

He looked a little deflated, "Okay, well, think about it."

Then he was pulling her toward the windows, pulling his shirt off. Then his shoes. "Think about it while you're teaching me how to fly, 'cause I suck at it."

She stepped out onto the platform overlooking its lush valley. It was beautiful, even though there looked to be places where the greenery had been hit by falling meteors, with entire swaths of trees destroyed. At her feet, there were loose pine needles and bits of broken wood and bark, clumps of dirt littering the stone.

She smiled. Her dragon chuckled.

He pulled her into his arms, lowering his lips to hers.

It felt like forever since the last time they had a moment to touch.

Her belly flopped, wrenching a gasp from her.

"What is it?"

She pulled his hand to her lower abdomen where it felt like their baby was doing barrel rolls in her belly, stealing her breath.

Jori's eyes widened, "Does it hurt?"

She shook her head, laughing, "Just strange."

Freeing herself of her own clothes, she smiled at Jori as they stepped closer to the ledge.

Turning toward him, her fingers slid up the warm skin over his ribs and abs. She looked down and smiled, licking her lips. "Let's see how far we can get for your first lesson, then we'll talk about this new life you're offering."

His voice was husky, "Or we can just stay here and finish what you just started."

She laughed, disengaging herself, and stepped back.

Her magic swarmed around her. The shell around the child tightened. She could fly for a little while. Her neon pink claws gripped the stone ledge, pulling Jori's attention. He was magnificent in his dragon form.

Her dragon agreed, as she gracefully launched herself into the sky, showing him how it was done.

More Dragon Island stories coming soon!

Read more paranormal romance with the *Global Paranormal Security Agency* series:

Kymri and Jori appear in urban fantasy story **Dragon Steel**, featuring Kolina Steelscale!

DRAGON STEEL

The world is changing and Kolina Steelscale must learn how to bend with it, or risk breaking her chance of a stronger future.

Read on for Chapter 1 of Dragon Steel...

Dragon Steel

Kolina Steelscale stood on the tower platform overlooking the island of Aeleftheria Nisi spread out before her. A collection of villages lay strung along the coastline, stretching inland and joining, until one city nestled against the base of the queen's citadel.

Dragon shifters and humans alike, all female, living and working together, maintaining the harmony of the archipelago civilization hidden in the vast Atlantic Ocean, deep in the region known to the rest of the world as the Bermuda Triangle.

She stood, hands resting behind her back with her fingers curled around a locket, feet planted shoulder-width apart, monitoring the comings and goings below, as well as the increased patrol progress above. Swallowing a lump in her throat, she straightened her spine, pushing away intrusive thoughts of her daughter.

That will do you no good, Kolina.

Three dark spots in the sky approached in a uniform arc, growing larger until Kolina could make out the shape of their wings, supporting their glittering scale-covered bodies through the air.

She rubbed a thumb over the etched surface of the locket in her grasp once more before tucking it into her pocket. She used the few seconds before they landed to tie her long, graying, dark hair back from her face.

They came in fast, and banked hard, pushing the air into chaotic eddies of turbulence that twisted across the open deck of the platform. Kolina closed her eyes against the kick-up of dust, but not before she caught the flash of color adorning the claws of the left-wing guardian.

The currents settled. She opened her eyes and raised a brow, but otherwise waited patiently for the three to land, shift from their dragon to human form, and grab their robes from the change room.

"Aunt Kolina," the one approaching addressed her.

Kolina looked pointedly at the color glittering on her finger and toenails, visible above her open-toed sandals. "I thought you and Kymri didn't get along."

Zayli snorted. "Cousin-rivalry. We may not get along *all* the time, but we're still kin." Besides, I miss her, and nail polish is her thing."

"You miss pushing her buttons," Kolina said, turning to walk along the parapet and not toward the inner guardian offices. "I suppose some of the others aren't making it easy for you?"

Zayli shrugged. "I ignore it." She followed Kolina around toward another platform on the south side of the tower.

"How is it out there?"

"You've read the reports."

Kolina nodded. "And?"

Zayli sighed. "It's storm season, so everyone's exhausted with the extra patrol duty. Tempers are flaring more than usual. I'm not telling you anything you don't already know, or anything more than I report to my commander. Why are you here?"

Kolina stopped walking at the blunt question.

"Has Marli returned to the island, or has anyone left to meet with her and Kymri?"

Zayli shook her head. "No one would dare, without Queen Regina's permission or command. What's going on?" She dropped her voice.

Kolina drew a deep breath, debating what to say to her niece—if anything at all. After a moment, she looked back toward the horizon and blew out a breath. "I don't know. At least, not yet."

"But something's wrong?" Zayli straightened, alert. "I haven't seen you concerned in a long time."

Kolina nodded. It wasn't something she could put a finger—or a claw—to. Not yet. It was a pitched vibration almost unnoticed. Almost. Like a dog whistle. Inaudible, but at the right pitch to slide under her scales and ride the nape of her neck.

"If you *feel* something, you'll tell me. Report it to your commander, of course, but report to me too. *Anything* out of place. Your commander won't ask it of the guardians under her orders. It isn't her style. But I want every dragoness, of every squad, reporting what they can't see, hear, taste or smell, too."

Zayli frowned. "Yes, aunt."

Kolina sighed and softened a fraction, reaching out her hand to touch her niece's shoulder; something that before Kymri's absence, she'd have never done.

Things had changed.

"I know there is a lot of tension between everyone. Between you and others, because of Kymri. Our duty to our queen's safety is above that."

Zayli snorted. "You don't have to tell *me* that. I know all about duty." She did nothing to mask the acid in her tone.

Kolina nodded.

Zayli was the one that always pushed the 'duty' line and had been right there supporting Kolina when she'd talked to Kymri about hers. "Is that all, Aunt?"

"Yes. Thank you."

Zayli turned at the next open archway leading toward the interior of the tower and strode down it in the direction of her quarters.

Offspring.

It was the one area of Kymri's life that she'd refused to fulfill.

And now, the long-standing peaceful island was struggling to keep from slipping into chaos.

Kymri's resistance to her duty to have young had pushed her into a heat that resulted in poor judgment choices.

Kolina sighed. She couldn't blame Kymri for the recent attacks from the male dragon tribe, but everyone else did. The object of her heat, Jori Mountainside, had unknowingly led them right to the island, threatening the safety of both the queen and the rest of the population.

Now, they were all on high alert to fend off more attacks from the much larger dragons.

More would come.

They all knew it.

And there'd been no more information from Kymri or Marli since Marli's sparse report arrived from the continent.

All they knew was that Kymri and Jori were alive, as was Elora—Jori's mother and the queen's trusted ambassador—who'd disappeared several decades before, and that the Dragon King was dead.

But that wouldn't stop his radicalized followers from carrying on his ideology and attacking the female-populated island to take control.

None of them would allow that to happen, but given how much larger male dragons were than female—it wouldn't be easy. The queen's guardians were all highly trained warriors. They'd die for their queen and people.

Why hasn't Kymri come back?

Kolina stepped into the frame of her long-time friend Launia's open office door.

Launia glanced up from the reports she scowled over, lips quirking at the corners. "I wondered how long before you graced my threshold."

"Well, you know, the queen likes to keep me busy." She brushed the hair from her face, tilting her nose toward the ceiling.

Launia snorted at Kolina's affectation of self-importance, reminding both of them of some of their island sorority. Her eyes twinkled, and the severity of the worry lines creasing her forehead eased. Then she raised a brow. "Are you here officially, or personally?"

"Both." Kolina closed the office door and approached Launia's desk, resting a haunch on the corner as she looked down at her friend and colleague.

Launia eased back in her seat, folding her hands across her lap as she eyed Kolina. "Reports are unchanged. The guardians are exhausted."

Kolina nodded. "I spoke to Zayli." She repeated what she asked of Zayli.

Launia's gaze narrowed on Kolina, worrying a lip as she considered her request.

"That bad, huh?"

"Maybe. That's the problem. I just don't know. The queen has been...different, since Kymri left. Everything feels different."

"Or you're not sleeping enough and are worrying about your youngling."

"Who isn't so young anymore. Not for a long time."

Launia snorted again, brow rising higher as she studied Kolina again.

Kolina sighed. "I know. You don't have to say it." Kolina knew full well how much she had interfered in Kymri's life.

And she was sure that was the reason Kymri had resisted her duty to produce offspring for so long, until her biology hadn't given her a choice.

Kymri: Independent, stubborn, loyal.

Gone.

For weeks now.

She stood, pacing the length of Launia's heavy, ornately carved wood desk. "This is all my fault. If I hadn't pushed Kymri so hard, she'd still be here, carrying her child in the safety of our island home, the male dragon tribe never having found us."

"Don't do that. Kolina, we all knew they'd find us one day. It was always just a matter of when. And Jori Mountainside's arrival would have happened regardless of any family squabbles between you and your daughter."

Kolina abruptly changed topics. "I can't believe Elora is alive."

Launia blinked, nodding. "And Odson never said a word about it. Maybe that's why the queen is unsettled."

Kolina's gaze darted back to Launia's face, heart twisting in her chest. "Odson Blackridge has always been a wild card." She considered the circumstances of his withholding that information for so long. "But I understand why he kept that secret from her—why Elora asked it of him."

Kolina knew too well what it was to have to make hard choices to protect a son, unwanted by their society.

Many of the dragonesses on this island did.

After Kolina left Launia's office, she walked the circumference of the island, studying the walled citadel, with its towers stretched skyward, looking for flaws in their defenses from below. The Queen's Spire soared above all the others, a beacon of the queen's presence on the island. The city surrounded the walls like a layered cloak down toward the uneven shoreline. Sailing ships buoyed in the harbor, fishing boats lined the smaller keys and docks.

Everything looked as it should.

And yet, Kolina couldn't shake her unease.

Was it just the effects of recent events and the revelation that the queen's longtime companion, Elora, was in fact still alive, after her disappearance from a diplomatic mission more than three decades ago?

Kolina extracted her locket from her pocket again, wrapping the chain over her fingers as she studied the etched surface. Its finely crafted face bore the insignia of an elite Aeleftherian guardian commander.

Its existence was shrouded from others most of the time. It usually lay out of sight, against her chest, under her clothing. Since events with Kymri and Jori, Kolina found herself reaching for it more and more, seeking the comfort of its solidity in her hands; what it represented.

Her thumb slipped over the image of the winged shield once more before she fastened the delicate chain's clasps behind her neck and tucked it back under her shirt.

With a sigh, she cast her gaze back across the horizon.

If the queen were deeply unsettled, the resonance of her magic could create the sense of island-wide unease.

But if there was something else, something dangerous causing it, then Kolina had to figure out what it was.

As a member of the Queen's Honor Guard, it was her duty to ensure the safety of their monarch, which ensured the safety of their small nation.

She surveyed the harbor. None of the ships were unfamiliar. The port master did her job as diligently as everyone else under the queen's rule.

Every dragoness that chose to live on the island did so with the full understanding of the queen's absolute rule and accepted the established laws for the protection of the tribe.

No one wanted to go back to life under the dominance of the male tribe.

No one.

Anyone that disagreed with the laws, left.

It had been more complicated than that for Elora. The queen's closest companion and loyal ambassador. She hadn't left the island with the purpose of abandoning her people. Just the opposite. She just hadn't come back.

Kolina had been in the queen's chambers during Odson Blackridge's retelling of Elora's story up to the point of her supposed second disappearance. What she'd endured in the claws of the Dragon King. And yet, she'd never given away the island's location to *him*.

But she had to her son. Covertly, yes. But she'd still given them that information.

Something Kolina had never done.

Her thoughts briefly flicked to the past, hit a wall of heartache and bounced back to the present. Her fingers brushed against the fabric of her shirt over the locket.

I need to fly.

She climbed back up to the nearest citadel gate and up higher still to the flight platforms.

Another rotation of guardians arrived and departed.

Near the platform jutting from the Queen's Tower, where her personal guard resided, Kolina stripped in the change room and made her way out to the ledge.

Several of her fellow Queen's Guard eyed her, their judgment plain on their faces.

Drawing her magic inward, the air around her shimmered and writhed. Her consciousness remained focused on the change as her body mass expanded until she stood on thick-padded talons. The metallic scales of her forelegs glittered under the tropical sun. Her body shimmered as she launched. Her wings snapped out and down, forcing her upward before they curled inward and pushed down again. And again, until she caught the higher currents, through gradient layers of blue sky.

Her shoulders settled with the old familiarity of the archipelago patrol route.

When Kymri was old enough to join the guardian patrols, Kolina had moved into her own mother's position in the Queen's Guard while her mother had stepped into the Queen's Council.

It was the way of things.

Kymri.

Would she come back? Surely, she would bring her youngling back to the island.

I've pushed her away.

She had bonded with Jori Mountainside. That changed everything. Complicated things beyond a simple heat.

A bond.

Kolina flew higher.

The patrols were visible off her wingtip. She wouldn't interrupt them.

She soared toward the small island at the farthest end of Draconia's archipelago, where Kymri had found Jori and his little plane, throwing everyone's lives into turmoil.

Find her.

Angling her nose toward the main island, she rode the currents home.

She had to review the transcripts of Marli's report.

A deep base tone rippled out from the citadel.

Every muscle in Kolina's body tensed, her head whipping in the direction of the sound.

An attack!

She slid her gaze across the vast horizon looking for the source of the threat.

There!

North of the island, a cluster of dark specks swarmed around itself.

Bringing her wings down with a hard push, she climbed the atmosphere, gaining height, and then speed when she angled herself and tilted her wings, turning herself into a giant snarling arrow.

Two attackers were being harried by three patrol guardians. Three wasn't enough, but more were coming.

One of the larger male dragons broke away from the cluster, angling downward, claws extended, toward the island. Not toward the citadel. The villages.

Kolina's heart leaped into her long throat. She knew every woman and child in those villages. She was close enough now to see them scurrying between the houses and shops seeking shelter. Most streamed toward the citadel. Others would go into their cellars or find other hiding places, but there wasn't enough time for everyone to find adequate shelter from a dragon, let alone a male dragon.

More guardians moved to intercept him, but not in time to stop him from razing a few small houses.

Kolina tilted, pulling her wings in tight, and dove. Holding her breath, she plunged faster and faster.

She roared, drawing the attention of the guardians attacking the destructive male, just in time for them to pull away. She adjusted her angle in the last seconds, colliding with him so hard the impact sent them both soaring back out toward the ocean.

The hit knocked the breath from her. Pain streaked through her shoulder, sharp and blinding. She held her focus long enough to get her claws into him so that the weight and momentum of her body would force him down into the water before his shock wore off.

In the water, she would be just as vulnerable. As soon as they stopped sinking, she pushed off from him, swimming to the surface before he could turn her tactics back on her.

His teeth grazed her tail from below.

She swung it, snapping him in the face with its tip, as she continued to force her way upward.

He lunged again, sinking his teeth into a thicker part of her tail. Her hind leg kicked out, claws tearing into his face, forcing him to release her.

Her head broke the surface and she dragged air into her lungs while using her forearms and hindquarters to propel herself toward shallow water so she could get back into the air. Pain spiked through her left shoulder with each movement.

Clouds of blood drifted through the ocean water around her. She couldn't tell if it was his or her own. She didn't care.

Guardians circled overhead, waiting for the male to reappear. The other male now had eight harrying guardians forcing him away from the island, their jaws snapping at him, trying to catch a wing or his tail, to force him down too.

Finally reaching the land shelf several miles down the shoreline from the closest village, she struggled to get back into the air. Pain flared through her shoulder when she flexed her wings.

Dragonsdammit!

Overhead, her sisters battled. Attack, counterattack, blocking the male's attempts to do more damage to the island and Aeleftheria's inhabitants.

They aren't taking anyone. They're here to destroy us.

The male she'd brought down into the water swam toward the smaller islands. His own cluster of guardians circled overhead, tracking his progress.

Her tail throbbed where his teeth had crushed through some of her scales and punctured her hide. Favoring her left foreleg, she limped to shore, her eyes on the action above.

The longer she stayed in her dragon form, the faster she would heal, but the pain made it difficult to hold the magic. The human part of her wanted to retreat into darkness, allowing oblivion to soothe the wounds. She stubbornly held her form, watching and listening with her keener dragon senses until the combatants were nothing more than swirling specks in the sky. Muted roars continued to roll across the surface of the ocean until they were indistinguishable from the waves crashing into the shoreline.

Still, she waited, in case they came back.

They didn't return.

She limped her way closer to the nearest village.

Finally, the guardian squads returned. One dragoness broke away from her small cluster.

Zayli.

Kolina let go of her magic, shrinking down to her human form. Her lower back throbbed, her shoulder screamed.

Zayli landed, then angled her wing to make room for Kolina to ride. She huffed impatiently.

Kolina was in too much pain, and too old, to let pride force her into a naked, head-held-high stroll back through the villages and up to the citadel to present herself to the shamans.

She struggled to climb her niece's foreleg to settle precariously on her back, clinging to her spikes without impaling herself. The trip took minutes.

Kolina slid off Zayli's neck into the care of several waiting shamans on the patrol platform closest to the infirmary.

READ MORE OF DRAGON STEEL AT:
https://jodikendrick.com/book/dragon-steel/

GPSA

While you wait for more Dragon Island stories...
Carson and Lirikai have their own story in *Awakened* – the first book of *The Aquatic Investigations* trilogy in *The Global Paranormal Security Agency* series!
(Awakened is free for newsletter subscribers at JodiKendrick.com)

The Global Paranormal Security Agency

The Global Paranormal Security Agency is a hidden organization dedicated to bridging the paranormal and human worlds to keep everyone safe.
Protect. Defend. Seek Justice.

jodikendrick.com/series/global-paranormal-security-agency/

Note to the Reader

Dear Reader,

Thank you so much for taking the time to read **_Dragon Heat_**! If you enjoyed it, please consider leaving a review on your favourite platform.

Dragon Heat was originally written for Milly Taiden's _Sassy Ever After_ series' spin-off **Draconia Island** project and published by MT Worlds Press in 2020.

Read all the books in this special release!

Dragon in Disguise by TB Mann
Dragon Princess: Treasured Love by Renee Hewett
Fire and Sass by Francis Rondon
Frost and Fangs by Scarlet Fox
My Mate's Rhythm by Terri A. Wilson
Walk the Sass by Julia Mills
Wings of Sass by Lia Davis
Dragon Heat by **Jodi Kendrick**

I hope you enjoyed it and are interested in reading more of my work.
-Jodi

About Jodi Kendrick

Jodi Kendrick lives in Eastern Ontario Canada with her *Favourite Person* and chompy furbaby, while their adult children explore the wider world.

As a romance author, she writes in paranormal, fantasy, steampunk & gaslamp subgenres, and sometimes delves into urban fantasy and paranormal women's fiction. Her characters are often quirky, sometimes cranky, but they all woman-up and get the job done while their partners ensure they survive with all their bits and bobs attached.

A history enthusiast and word dabbler most of her life, she enjoys exploring 'beyond-the-everyday' and the 'time-before-now', discovering relationship threads weaving individuals through time and place. She's rarely seen without flashy notebooks and colourful pens.

Follow Jodi on Social Media:

Dragon Island
Dragon Heat

Enchanted Ardor
Wish

EveL Worlds : FUCN'A
Tough Nut
Diamond in the Ruff
Honeyed Nut
Gorilla in the Hiss
FUCN'A Collection One
Pedigree Collection

Finely Aged
Dragon Steel

Global Paranormal Security Agency
Awakened
Surfacing
Polestar
Aquatic Investigations
Prowler

The Kindred Chronicles
Healer
Mercenary

The Soaring Dragon Chronicles
Return Flight
Changeling